Wendy Haynes

Saving Hollow Woods

Book One: The Door in the Woods

An Inprint Publishing book.

Published by Inprint Publishing

8a Maysfield Circuit, Port Macquarie, NSW 2444

www.inprintpublishing.com.au

First published by Inprint Publishing August 2020

Copyright © Wendy Haynes 2020

Cover Design by Annie Seaton

The moral rights of the author have been asserted.

All rights reserved: no part of this publication can be reproduced or transmitted by any means, electronic, mechanical, including photocopying (except under the statutory exceptions provisions of the Australian *Copyright Act 1968),* recording, scanning or by any information storage and retrieval system without the prior written permission of Inprint Publishing.

 A catalogue record for this books is available from the National Library of Australia

ISBN 978 0 98764 351 3

DEDICATION

To my grandchildren Brielle, Michala and Cooper anything is possible in life. Just reach out and grab it.

WENDY HAYNES

'*The Door in the Woods* series is reminiscent of Enid Blyton's *The Enchanted Wood*, with all the joy, adventure, magic, and danger of a children's fantasy adventure. Highly recommended for readers 8-12!'
-Hayley Lawrence-

Thank you to my beta readers – Mia, Isaac, and Cameron.

Chapter 1

'Can't you be quiet for just ten minutes? It's noisy enough on this train,' Gertrude said to the boy sitting opposite her.

'Of course, I can.' Tristan stood, drew in some air, and clamped his mouth shut. He was starting to go red in the face, and a white tinge appeared around his mouth and blond eyebrows.

This was the first time Gertrude had seen the country, being a city girl. The countryside flashed by in different shades of lush green as the afternoon sun made its way to the bottom of the horizon.

'You don't have to stop breathing to be quiet, silly,' she said with a chuckle.

Tristan blew out, and then inhaled deeply, bringing his breath back to normal.

'I know, but it was funny, wasn't it? It made you laugh.'

Tristan's clothes were rather bedraggled, and his blond hair stuck to his head from lack of washing. He was a few inches taller than Gertrude. And, as thin as a wafer with piercing blue eyes.

'My name is Gertrude, what's yours?' Gertrude offered her hand for the boy to shake.

He wiped his dirt-smudged hands down his clothes. 'I'm Tristan the Adventurer,' he announced, with a smile on his face as he grasped Gertrude's hand.

'How can you be an adventurer? You're just a boy.'

'I'm always on an adventure. But before long I'll end up back at the orphanage.' The smile disappeared from his face.

Gertrude sank back into the leather bench seat. Her mass of red curls bounced as she wriggled to get comfortable. She wore a tartan skirt with a once-white blouse, and an oversized shabby grey cardigan the governess had given her. Like Tristan's, her clothes were stained and dotted with holes.

'Oh, isn't that strange? I'm from the orphanage for girls. You know, the one on the east side of Britania? We were only a block away from the bombing last week. Many people have already left Britania. Where're your papers? Let me have a look.'

Tristan handed his papers to Gertrude, who he thought was rather bossy. She pulled her papers out of her pocket to compare them. As she read the documents, she discovered they were the same age, twelve.

'Ah-ha, just as I suspected. We're going to the same county.'

'Really? That's different. No one has ever gone to the same place as me before.'

'How many adventures have you been on?'

'Six.'

'That many, what happened?'

Tristan shook his head. 'I don't know.' Frowning, he flopped down on the seat opposite Gertrude. 'Nobody seems to want me.' He shrugged.

Gertrude wondered if she was going to the same place as Tristan, whether she too would be sent back to the orphanage. One day in that place was enough for anyone. She'd spent six months at the orphanage after she lost sight of her parents when the bombing began. It was awful. People scattering every which way. Dust and smoke filled the air. Gertrude's mother was holding her hand but in the confusion her parents had just disappeared.

She couldn't understand why a country would decide to start a war and try and take over another country. And it had gotten to the point that most of the children in the orphanages were either shoved out on the street to fend for themselves or farmed off to the country. She was eager to stay as far away from the orphanage as possible.

In her heart, Gertrude believed her parents were alive despite what the governess had to say. And

Gertrude worried that although she was escaping the orphanage, it would make it harder for her parents to find her.

They were seated in a private compartment in the fourth carriage from the engine. Most of the other carriages were full of people hanging out of the windows, waving goodbye to their loved ones. Gertrude and Tristan had been ushered to their compartment when they had boarded the train. All Gertrude knew, she was on a long journey to a place that she had never heard of. Oakvale sounded like a nice place. But who was waiting for her and Tristan at the other end? Were they going to the same ward? And why was Tristan being sent back to the orphanage over and over again?

Their small amount of tattered luggage had been stowed in the racks overhead by the conductor. He had warned them to behave, or they would be out on their ear, at the next stop. He had then slammed the door behind him. Gertrude could hear him as he bustled about bossing everyone he came across. She made a mental note not to leave the compartment unless necessary.

Her journey had begun at Britania Station, a place she knew so well. From the time she could walk, she had been catching trains from that station with her mother.

'Hey, look,' said Tristan, pointing to a mob of sheep being rounded up by a dog and a farmer on a horse. His nose was squashed against the glass window. 'I wish I could ride a horse. He fumbled in his pocket, pulled out a dry crumbling biscuit, and took a bite.

'I've been looking forward to this all day. Who knows when our next meal will be.' Spittle and crumbs flew out of his mouth, landing on the glass.

'I'm sure whoever meets us, if indeed it is the same person at Oakvale, will realise that we would need to be fed. Maybe you should keep it just in case.'

Gertrude was feeling a bit peckish herself and wondered the same thing.

She was often hungry. The kind of food served up at the orphanage wasn't something that induced an appetite. One meal a day was the allowance, no exception. It usually consisted of undercooked watered-down oats, and the occasional day or two-old bread. Gertrude hoped she could have two meals a day, no laundry or cooking duties, and a clean bed with no lice.

Who would take in two children anyway, and why? I hope they're nice, she thought.

'Next stop Oakvale,' the conductor yelled, as he walked up and down the corridor. He slid the door to the compartment open, 'Hey, you kids. Grab your bags and be ready to jump off the train,' he said in a gruff voice.

Gertrude took a deep breath, stood, and braced herself for the jolting stop as the train slowed and neared the station.

There weren't many people waiting on the platform to greet them. An old lady with a straw hat stood beside the ticket office, and a middle-aged man in a business suit sat reading a newspaper. Another man with a bald head was walking away from the train, and a couple of ladies sat on a wooden bench knitting. Gertrude crossed her fingers and wished that whoever was standing out there, it would all turn out just as it was supposed to.

Chapter 2

Gertrude and Tristan stepped off the train. The old lady in the straw hat looked at them anxiously as she walked towards them. Gertrude noticed her eyes; even though her forehead was wrinkled in a frown, her eyes were smiling, a good sign. The lady wasn't tall and was a bit on the plump side. She walked with a slight waddle. The strands of hair about her face were grey.

'Hello, children,' she said as Gertrude and Tristan made their way along the platform.

'This must be her,' Tristan whispered behind his hand.

Gertrude tried to smile at the stranger as she whispered a warning to Tristan, 'don't mess this one up.'

'Are you Tristan and Gertrude?'

'Yes,' they both said.

'I'm your new ward, Mrs Appleton. But you can call me Aunt Betty.

Gertrude moved forward. 'Hello, um Aunt Betty. I'm Gertrude.' She curtsied and shook Aunt Betty's hand.

'And I'm Tristan.' Tristan got confused about which hand to offer to Aunt Betty to shake, so he gave her both.

Gertrude rolled her eyes and bit her bottom lip. But Aunt Betty just let out a great big belly laugh, rubbed his head, and then took his hands.

'Come on, you two, you must be tired and hungry.' She led them to the end of the platform and out through the exit.

'Did your governesses tell you much about my place? Well, your place now.'

They both shook their heads.

'That's okay. You'll see it for yourselves. Let's get you home.'

'I won't be staying long. My parents will soon find me,' Gertrude responded.

'Oh my,' said Aunt Betty with a worried look forming on her face. 'Well, this is home for now.'

An old pickup truck sat outside the entrance to the railway station, and an even older man sat in the driver's seat. The truck was a rusty shade of brown. A few bales of hay rested against the back window.

'This is Mr. James, he's, my neighbour. I don't own a motor car, and he offered to help me get you children back to the farm.'

'A farm how, exciting,' said Tristan.

Gertrude elbowed him and told him to shush.

'You children will have to ride in the back,' said Mr. James.

They looked at each other and smiled. This was going to be fun.

'Have you been to a farm?' Gertrude asked Tristan as they heaved their bags into the truck and climbed in.

'No, never. This is definitely a different adventure?'

Gertrude hoped so for both their sakes.

They watched the beautiful green rolling hills and

valleys go by. Cows mooed as they passed, and they laughed. The gravel road made the trip a bit uncomfortable, but they didn't care; they were heading to their new home. Gertrude thought that perhaps this was the start of a wonderful adventure, for a while at least. Or if Tristan did whatever it was that he usually did, it might end within days. She would have to keep an eye on him.

As the truck slowed down, Gertrude and Tristan stood hanging on to the bar above the hay bales. Gertrude's red curls danced as the wind touched her face. The entrance to the farm was overgrown with long grass and weeds. The sign on the gate said, 'The Appleton Farm.' There were broken fence rails on either side of the driveway and a lot of potholes that bounced the children around. Gertrude almost lost her grip.

Everything looked old; the house had a large wooden veranda with a line of pots placed along the edge. An array of different flowers waved in the breeze. Over to the left a tractor sat beside a large wooden barn.

Tristan pointed to the tractor. 'Does it work,' he asked as he jumped out of the back of the truck.

'Why yes, it does, young man and Mr. James has kindly offered to show you around the farm tomorrow and get you acquainted with your chores.'

'Chores. Bu—'

'No buts, young man. Once you and Mr. James have things up and running, it shouldn't be hard for you to run the farm.'

'Run the farm! Oh, but what about school?' said Tristan.

'It seems because of the war; all schools will be closed. I will teach you what you need to know, I have a good understanding of the English language, and I've kept the books for this farm from the day I married Mr. Appleton, rest his soul.'

'What about me?' Gertrude piped up as they climbed the rickety wooden step onto the veranda.

'Well, little miss, you will be helping me mainly with the inside chores. Oh, and milking old Carmel. And, of course, collecting the eggs.'

Gertrude and Tristan looked at each other pulling

grim faces as they followed Aunt Betty into the house.

'She's going to make us into slaves,' whispered Tristan.

Chapter 3

'Where's my dungeon?' asked Tristan as Aunt Betty ushered them through the squeaky front door. Gertrude nudged him to mind his manners.

Tristan knew the drill; it would only be a matter of days before the old lady sent him on his way. Deep down, he wished this would be the one. He liked the idea of living on a farm. But how many chores were they expected to do? Having lived in the orphanage from the time he was born, cramped up in a small damp room with nothing he could call his own, this place seemed like heaven.

'This is your room, Tristan dear. I hope you like it. Tristan opened the large wooden door.

'Are you sure? I mean it's rather nice.' Tristan sat on the bed, and bounced, it felt so comfortable.

'Wow, a soft mattress! And look Gertrude, I have a window with a view,' he said, pushing the window up to let in the clean country air. 'Oh, and look, a dresser with a mirror. I've never had a mirror before. Golly gosh, is that how I look?'

'Thank you, Aunt Betty,' Tristan ran to her and hugged her tight.

'Oh, dear boy, you are welcome,' she said. A tear slipped down her cheek.

'Now it's your turn, young lady.' A little further down the hall was Gertrude's room. The window in her room faced the same way as Tristan's. Tristan could tell that this nice old lady had gone to some effort to decorate their rooms and make them feel welcome.

In the middle of Gertrude's room stood a four-poster bed with a lace canopy. The bed had a thick comfy-looking light green bedspread and plump pillows; she also had a dresser with a mirror. The last time Gertrude had slept in a bed, or even in a bedroom this size, was before her parents had vanished during the bombing raid.

'These rooms are like luxury hotel rooms, not like a dungeon at all. Sorry,' said Tristan.

'No harm done. I'm glad you like your rooms. I'll leave you both to get settled, I'll be in the kitchen getting you something to eat.'

Tristan was hungry; he had finished his morsel of biscuit on the train. He went back into his room and sat on the dark blue oval mat in the middle of his room. The same colour curtains hung at the window. The dresser was made of dark wood and had a toy truck sitting on top. He'd never owned a toy before. To the right of the window stood a desk and chair, and a cupboard on the opposite wall. A small set of drawers sat next to his new comfortable bed, with a bedspread in a lighter blue.

He was looking forward to bedtime for once. This seemed so different from his other adventures, but should he get his hopes up? Maybe it's a sign that this was where he was supposed to be. After all, Gertrude was with him, that was different.

***

On the table in the middle of the kitchen lay a basket

of freshly baked scones. Tristan had never tasted a scone before and groaned with pleasure with each mouthful.

Gertrude watched as Tristan slopped on a generous amount of jam and cream, which now appeared around his mouth like froth.

Tristan had noticed that Gertrude was eating hers with a similar eager appetite. He wondered if like him, Gertrude wanted to have a real home. Her hopes that one day her parents would find her were ludicrous, he thought. They had been gone too long.

'These are delicious,' he said, with the food still bulging to one side of his mouth. He grabbed another scone like a hungry dog.

'That's good, dear, but perhaps wait until you have finished what you are eating before you talk,' suggested Aunt Betty. He also received a warning glare from Gertrude.

'Why don't you finish up here and have a look around outside. Be in before dark,' said Aunt Betty.

Tristan raised his eyebrow to Gertrude, as if to say, so far so good. He always tried to come across as positive but the last two adventures, if you could call them that, had been disastrous.

Tristan had always been clumsy, especially in new surroundings. He knew this of himself, and he tried to be careful, but he couldn't stop things from happening.

At one of the homes he was sent to, he had been asked to light the fire, something he had done plenty of times at the orphanage when it was permitted. But this time the fire he lit set the curtains and antique settee up in flames. He was swiftly shoved out the door by the burly man of the house cursing him all the way back to the train station.

'Come on,' he said to Gertrude, as he grabbed another scone, shoved it in his pocket, and headed out the back of the house.

Chapter 4

Gertrude woke with a start the next morning as a constant ringing filled her room. She pulled the pillow over her head. It felt like she had slept on a cloud, floating and free. Her bed was so soft. The last time she slept in a bed was at home. The beginning of the morning sun crept through the gap in the curtains throwing a gentle strip of light across the wooden floor.

'Wake up, sleepyhead,' Aunt Betty said as she gently rocked Gertrude. 'It's time for a cup of hot chocolate and then the milking.'

'You can't be serious. It's too early.'

'It's on dawn, and Carmel gets milked first thing. Then she's out in the field for the day. Come on, Gertrude dear, I promise you will love it.'

Gertrude groaned and stretched as she sat up on the edge of her bed.

'Why isn't Tristan up?'

'Don't you worry yourself about him; he has plenty of work in front of him today. Put some old clothes on, dear, you might get a bit grubby.'

Gertrude waited for the door to close and rummaged through what few clothes she had in her bag. It didn't really matter what she wore, they were rags anyway. She picked out a pair of tattered navy pants, a faded green top and threw on her only jumper, where holes had multiplied each day. As she passed Tristan's room, she could hear him blissful snore. So, she tapped on the door a few times and ran for the kitchen.

'Sit down, Gertrude dear, and drink your hot chocolate. I'll put the scones in the oven for when we come back inside.'

She sat at a long wooden table which stood in the centre of the kitchen. The old stove was made of cast iron. Aunt Betty kept feeding it wood, which it gobbled up and roared to life. It made the room cosy against the last of the winter chill. The walls were an off-white, dulled from years of neglect. The windows were dressed in sheer lace to let in the warmth of the morning sun, which was peeking over the ridge in the distance. Gertrude hugged the cup of hot chocolate with her hands; it was delicious. She had almost forgotten what it tasted like.

The food she had been served at the orphanage — if you could call it food—had slopped around in the bowl and was tasteless. The hot chocolate reminded her of her mother. The times they had spent together cuddled up on the sofa on cold winter nights, talking and watching the flames of the fire dance in the fireplace. She missed her so much.

'Come on dear, Carmel is waiting.' Aunt Betty opened the back door.

Sure enough, as they made their way to the barn, Carmel started mooing. She was saying good morning. Aunt Betty lit a lamp that hung just above Carmel's stall. The light of the rising sun hadn't reached the inside of the barn.

It's huge, thought Gertrude as she looked about

the barn. Over to one side a stack of hay bales were piled four deep and about seven bales high. On the other side, next to Carmel were five more stalls. To the far end of the barn was a workbench and an array of tools hanging on the wall. That would probably be Tristan's domain, Gertrude smirked to herself. Though, she had done some tinkering with her father. They had constructed a cart to carry Gertrude's toys while she played.

'Why do you only have one cow?'

'Well, when Mr. Appleton passed away, there wasn't anyone else here to milk the cows. Mr. James from next door came and milked the other cows until I sold them. Besides, Carmel will give us enough milk. Grab that stool and bring it here, please dear,' she said, pointing to a three-legged wooden stool behind her. 'Have you milked a cow before?'

'No,' Gertrude said, shaking her head. She had never stood this close to an animal of Carmel's size, and by the look of Carmel, she had been eating a bit too much grass.

'Gertrude dear, just listen to my instruction, and

you'll see how easy this is. First, I always have a talk to Carmel, it soothes her. Go on, say hello.'

'Good morning, Carmel. Isn't it a beautiful morning?'

'That's wonderful, dear, I think you and Carmel will get on perfectly.'

'Moo...moo.'

'See, now she is saying hello too. Sit down on the stool and put your hands under the udder.' Aunt Betty squatted beside her and placed her own hands over Gertrude's and moved them in an up and down motion. Then she placed the bucket under the cow and began to help Gertrude milk Carmel.

'Oh look,' Gertrude said, in surprise and wonder. 'It's working.'

'Well, of course, it's working,' Aunt Betty said, with a smile on her face.

'Now you try it.' Aunt Betty let go of Gertrude's hands. Gertrude milked Carmel all by herself. She smiled up at her new guardian and giggled as Carmel let out another moo. It didn't take long to finish the milking. And then Gertrude lead Carmel, her new friend, out to a grassy field for the day.

On the way back to the house Aunt Betty let the chickens out of their coop. They scurried about as she threw grain on the ground. Gertrude and Aunt Betty collected ten eggs from ten chickens. Gertrude nestled the eggs in the front of her jumper and carried them back to the house.

'Let's see how those scones are going.'

'Can we have them now?'

'Oh no, not now. They're for morning tea. What about some porridge?'

'That sounds marvellous, I'm starving.'

Chapter 5

'Tristan,' yelled Gertrude. She ran towards him, and the broken fence. 'If you keep that up, we'll both end up back at the orphanage.' Ever since they'd arrived at the Appleton farm, every time Gertrude turned her back, anything Tristan touched got wrecked. She was starting to understand why he had returned from so many adventures, as he called them. Just at breakfast that morning, he'd spilled the jug of milk over the table. And like a domino effect, the milk jug hit the sugar bowl, and in careered onto the floor into a mixture of sugar with broken glass on the floor.

Aunt Betty got up, brushed up the mess, and said, 'dear me, you are rather clumsy.'

'She won't send us back. She needs us,' Tristan

said. He dismounted the idle tractor.

'How can you be so sure?' Gertrude paced back and forth in the knee-deep grass.

'Anyway. Mr. James said the fences needed fixing. So, no harm was done.'

'Fixing, not ploughing down.' Gertrude shook her head. She had barely arrived and Tristan, well, he seemed such a worry. She made her way back to the house, lifting her legs high through the thick grass.

Turning the tractor engine off, Tristan followed in her path.

Aunt Betty stood anxiously on the veranda. 'Well, my dear boy. Perhaps a few more lessons in the larger field will see fewer fences mowed down.'

Tristan mounted the step, hung his head as if waiting for something else to be said. But Aunt Betty just stood there.

'I'll go and pack my bag, shall I,' Tristan said. He gnawed at his bottom lip as he spoke.

'Now why on earth would you do that?' Aunt Betty lifted Tristan's head for him to look at her.

'I spilled the milk, I broke the sugar bowl, and

now, I ploughed down the fence,' he said, shifting from foot to foot.

The more he said, the more Gertrude worried about what would happen next. Was Tristan, right? Does Aunt Betty need them? Or were his antics going to send them back?

But Aunt Betty let out a deep belly laugh. They both looked at each other, then back at Aunt Betty, who now, with a serious look on her face, said, 'that's nothing to what I did last a few weeks ago. I dropped five eggs on the kitchen floor. Half of the goo landed in my slippers. I spilled most of the milk in the chicken's water tray on the way back from the barn, and set fire to the curtain in my bedroom.'

A smirked appeared on Tristan's face which soon turned into a giggle.

Before too long they were all laughing.

Gertrude suspected Aunt Betty had only said that to make Tristan feel at home. From that moment on, Gertrude knew they were both there to stay.

Gertrude soon had a regular routine. Waking early to milk Carmel and collecting the eggs. And helping

Aunt Betty weed the overgrown gardens that surround the house. She enjoyed the start of a new day, the stillness of it. And Carmel always mooed with delight when she heard Gertrude walking towards the barn.

Tristan, after flattening a few more fences, had finally got the knack of riding the tractor. With Mr. James' help he ploughed and planted potatoes in one of the fields.

Helping with the chores wasn't that bad after all. Gertrude noticed that Tristan wasn't nearly as clumsy as before. He had been nervous, worried, and tried too hard and that was what made him clumsy. Either way, things were looking brighter than they had in a long time.

Chapter 6

'Please, Aunt Betty,' Tristan begged. 'I'll stay here and do anything. Any chores that need doing. Even clean out Carmel's muck in her stall. Just as long as I don't have to go to church?'

'Now Tristan, my dear boy. We've had this conversation before and complaining about spending time with the Lord Almighty once a week, I just won't tolerate it. Now mind your tongue and tuck in your shirt.'

Gertrude raised her eyebrow at him. 'Tristan.'

'What?'

'You know what?'

He ignored Gertrude and waved to Mr. James as he came through the gates. The early morning breeze tugged gently at Gertrude's new turquoise dress. She had two new dresses for church. Tristan wore a stiff white shirt tucked into a pair of light grey trousers held up by a black belt. They both admired their new clothes and were thankful to have something decent to wear besides their old rags.

'Good morning to you, Mrs. Appleton. Morning, children. Jump in the back while I open the door for Mrs. Appleton,' Mr. James said as he stepped out of the truck.

Tristan jumped swiftly into the back. Gertrude stood assessing exactly how she was supposed to climb up onto the back of the truck with a dress on.

Aunt Betty noticed her struggle and sent Mr. James to her rescue. Gertrude much preferred the overall Aunt Betty had given them to wear while working on the farm. But she had to talk Aunty Betty around, explaining the practical side to wearing something a boy would typically wear.

'There you go, lass,' Mr. James said lifting Gertrude onto the bale of hay. The back tray of a truck wasn't practical for a girl with a dress. Gertrude held her dress down with one hand, and with the other hand she held on tight as they headed down the bumpy road into town.

'Now you two, if you behave yourselves, you'll free to wander for the afternoon,' said Aunt Betty. They were parked in front of the church. This was the second time they had attended. Gertrude was amazed at how many people showed up considering she never saw anyone come to the farm except for Mr. James. They all seemed to know each other well.

'I'll be good.' Gertrude said. 'What about you, Tristan?'

'Of course, I will.' He rolled his eyes and poked out his tongue.

'Come on then. The service is about to start.' They walked into the church together holding Aunt Betty's hand.

Even though the church service seemed to take forever, Gertrude didn't mind going to church. She enjoyed singing some of the hymns. She had been a member of the choir at school before her world had been turned upside down. She used this time to remind God where she was. So, her mother and father could find her.

They sat close to the front, the second row in the middle. The pastor was a tall narrow fellow with a goat-like beard. He wore a white shin-length robe. His voice was as narrow as he was. There was no rise and fall in tone or volume. Which for Gertrude made the service seem to drag on.

Aunt Betty sang loads of songs, on key most of the time. And blended in with the chortling voices of the congregation nicely. Gertrude knew after two visits to the church when the money tray went around, the service would soon be over.

After church, Aunt Betty got bailed up by one of the church committee members asking her to make pickles for the next bazaar. Gertrude was eager, as was Tristan, to get home, have lunch and go exploring.

***

'Now go change out of your church clothes. And make sure you hang them up. You can get another wear or two out of them before they need washing. I'll have lunch for you shortly.'

'What's for lunch, Aunt Betty?' asked Tristan.

'Pea and ham soup with bread. I made it last night.'

'Ummm,' sounded Tristan and he raced off to change his clothes.

Tristan sat opposite Gertrude slurping his soup and dipping big chunks of bread into it.

'There is no hurry, you know. It's not your last meal,' said Gertrude.

'But it's delicious.'

'Mind your manners, dear. Less noise would be preferred,' said Aunt Betty.

The children cleared the table putting their empty bowls on the sink.

'Go on, you two. Go and enjoy the outdoors for a while. Be back before dark.'

'Yes, Aunt Betty,' they replied.

Gertrude hadn't been any further than the field where Carmel grazed each day. The Appleton Farm was large. It was greater than the eye could see and backed onto the woods on the east side of the property.

Before Gertrude left, she asked with a slight

grimace. 'Aunt Betty, would you mind terribly much, writing to the orphanage soon. I don't mean to offend you, but I want to make sure my parents can find me.'

'I will write a letter this afternoon after my afternoon nap.'

'Thank you.'

Tristan took off in the direction of the brook which ran right through the property. He carried a fishing rod given to him by Mr. James.

Gertrude went for a walk in the field. She said hello to Carmel. She could tell that Carmel was glad to see her. The cow mooed as she got closer. Gertrude wore her overalls and lifted her legs high to wade through the grass in the field. The field was lush and green with plenty more feed for Carmel to devour. Carmel was quite old, and she had a lovely nature. As Gertrude petted her, the cow rubbed against her eager for it to continue. Aunt Betty had told Gertrude Carmel could spend a month in the field before she would be moved to the next one.

Not too far away, two fields over, Gertrude could

see a large group of trees. The trees canopies were waving in the slight breeze. 'I'll be back soon Carmel.' She gave the cow a kiss on her cheek.

Chapter 7

The grass got thicker as Gertrude made her way to the entrance to the woods. Gertrude had to lift her legs even higher to get through it. She felt like she was marching in a band. Looking back; she could still see the house. She pulled the wire on the fence down which led to the next field and ducked through. It took her a good fifteen minutes to walk from one side to the other. She hurdled the second fence and made her way to the clump of trees.

The trees looked like willows and seemed longstanding. Gertrude sat under the shade of the first tree getting her breath back, wishing she had brought some water. It was very dark under the canopy of the trees, and the breeze pushed the trees back and forth as if they were moving to music. The sound was haunting. And now that she was there, she wondered whether she should go any further.

Don't be a chicken, Gertrude, this was nothing compared to the orphanage. And with that, she crept through the trees. They brushed her head and neck with their fingers; and it tickled. As she walked further and further into the woods, her heartbeat faster, and faster. She wished, like Hansel and Gretel, she had brought something to guide her way back.

She was heading into darkness; it wasn't fun anymore. It was scary. The sun spread fingers of dim light between the trees. All the noises of the forest became louder. Every sound made Gertrude jolt to a stop and listen. She spun around but nothing was there.

She decided to turn around and head home. She didn't want to spend her afternoon in the spooky woods. On the way back she noticed this massive tree with large branches sweeping down to the floor of the woods. The trunk was covered with vines. But when the sun's rays filtered through the canopy, she could see something shining. She pulled the vines aside, ripping at them. Buried deep behind the vines she discovered a large round door knocker, bigger than her hand. She heaved at another handful of vines to get a closer look. Gertrude realised the knocker was attached to a door.

Why would a door be in a tree trunk? How did it get there? And what is behind it?

There was only one way to find out. She grabbed the knocker and turned it to the left, and right, but all she heard was a creaking sound. It would not budge. She pushed on the door with all her might.

But nothing.

It seemed to be getting darker now. Perhaps there were clouds above. Gertrude couldn't really tell under the thickness of the trees. So, she covered the door up as best she could. She looked around for something she could use to mark the spot. There was a large boulder to the left of the door. But how would she find the door again from the edge of the woods? She had to know where that door led to.

What was inside?

She gathered a handful of small rocks and made a trail back the way she came or so she thought.

When she came out of the woods the house wasn't visible.

Oh no, I'm lost! She moved further into the field and looked in every direction. She couldn't see the house. She didn't know whether to walk to the left or the right.

She scanned the area for a landmark. And just below one of the trees on the edge of the woods was a group of mushrooms. But all the trees looked exactly the same.

No, that won't do. Then she spied an old wooden fence post peeking out of some shrubs closer to the field. She dragged the post into position at the mouth of the trail. Satisfied, she took her first route to the left. She resolved if she counted five hundred steps to the left and couldn't see the farmhouse, she would turn around and walk 1000 steps to the right. '331, 332,334.' Gertrude looked up at the darkening sky and saw smoke, which could only be coming from Aunt Betty's chimney.

Chapter 8

'Well, my dear, what have you been up to? You're filthy,' said Aunt Betty.

Gertrude looked down at her clothes and discovered they were smudged with dirt. Gertrude didn't want to lie to Aunt Betty. But even if she told her the truth, Aunt Betty wouldn't believe her; who would? After all who's ever found a door in a tree trunk in the woods.

'Um I was playing with Carmel for a while, and she got a bit frisky and started chasing me. So, I ran and then fell in a dirt patch in the field,' she lied.

'Alright, dear. You better go and have a scrub before supper.'

Gertrude turned from the kitchen to enter the hall and almost knocked Tristan over.

'Watch out silly, what are you doing standing

there?'

'Listening to you lie.'

'What?'

'You heard me.'

'Keep your voice down,' said Gertrude, dragging Tristan into her room.

'So where were you really?'

'Aunt Betty told me to have my bath, I'll tell you after that.'

'No, tell me now, or I'm telling.'

'Okay. But you won't believe me?'

Gertrude sat on the floor in the middle of her room and indicated to Tristan to close the door.

'Well?' he said, plonking himself on the floor opposite her.

'It's hard to explain.'

'Try me.'

Gertrude recapped her afternoon, and after explaining the door in the tree, Tristan burst into laughter.

'Shh Tristan, it's true.'

'That's some imagination you have there.' Still

laughing, he left the room.

Tristan didn't know it, but Gertrude had a plan. That night she waited until the house was quiet and everyone was asleep, and she slipped out of bed. Her bedroom door squeaked as she opened it, and she made a mental note to grease it the next day. The floorboards creaked underfoot with each step she took, which made walking the length of the hall a slow process indeed. She finally reached the kitchen and opened the bottom drawer and felt for the torch.

'What are you doing?'

Gertrude almost screamed and put her hand over her mouth to stop it. 'Tristan, you scared me,' she said in a hushed voice.

'Well, what are you doing with that torch?'

'I couldn't sleep. I want to know what's behind that door.'

'Well, I'm coming with you.'

'You didn't believe me,' she said putting her hands on her hips.

'But I'm still coming,' Tristan retaliated. But before they had a chance to do anything Aunt Betty called out from her room and said, 'get what you need and go back to bed.'

'Yes, Aunt Betty' was the reply they gave, and scurried back to their rooms.

What now?

Gertrude would feel safer if Tristan was with her when she went back to the woods. The Woods were creepy, even in the daylight. Going to the woods by herself in the middle of the night wasn't one of her best ideas, she was sure. *What was I thinking?*

She was curious mostly, and was glad Tristan caught her. Gertrude lay in bed not able to sleep and she would plan a trip back to the door with Tristan in the morning.

They had an afternoon off from lessons on account of them doing so well with their arithmetic lesson in the morning. Gertrude grabbed the torch she had hidden under her pillow the night before and stuffed it in the folds of her oversized jumper.

Aunt Betty was busy cooking pickles for the church bazaar. 'Have a lovely afternoon my dears, and—'

'We know. Be back before dark,' Tristan interrupted.

'Yes,' she said turning back to the tomatoes simmering on the cooktop. Once passed the barn, Gertrude said, 'we need to head back no later than four o'clock. Aunt Betty would be cross with us and might not let us out for who knows how long, alright?'

Tristan nodded agreement. They marched together towards the woods. Gertrude reminded Tristan last time he was late Aunt Betty tapped on her watch and had told him not to be tardy with his time, sending him to his room for three whole hours.

Gertrude knew if she circled the woods, she would find the old fence post she had left there. It was hard to know if she walked the same trail back to the woods. When she was close enough, she started counting.

'What are you doing?'

'Counting silly.'

Tristan shook his head bemused and followed behind.

'Here, look. The post.' She looked at Tristan and a smile started to form, and he grinned back. 'Come on this way.'

'It looks pretty dark in here.'

'It'll be alright. Come on it's not much further now.'

Gertrude was acting brave. She was having second thoughts herself, about walking through the creepy woods. She turned on the torch, aiming it at the ground. She was searching for the small rock she had dropped the day before to guide her back to the door in the tree trunk.

'What if there is a monster behind the door?' Tristan asked.

'Well, we will run all the way back home. Stop it, you're scaring me.'

'Who puts a door in a tree in the woods anyway?' Just at that moment, a large, winged creature flew in front of them, and they both fell backward.

'What was that?' said Tristan.

'I'm...not sure,' said Gertrude, feeling for Tristan's hand after they had brushed themselves off. 'Look,

Tristan. There it is. I told you.'

'Wow. That is stranger than strange. A door in a tree? Let's go in.'

Gertrude gave Tristan a sideways look and knocked on the door. 'It's polite to knock.' The noise boomed through the woods and echoed. But nothing happened.

'Try opening it,' suggested Tristan. Gertrude turned the large metal knocker to the left and pushed. And then to the right. But it wouldn't budge.

'Here, give me a go,' said Tristan. He pushed and pulled at the door. The door creaked from the strain. He tried tugging the brass ring to the left and then to the right which left him huffing and puffing.

'See, it won't open,' said Gertrude.

'Let's try it tomorrow.'

Chapter 9

'Come on, Gertrude. Carmel won't milk herself,' said Aunt Betty as she opened Gertrude's bedroom door on her way to the kitchen. All Gertrude wanted to do was stay in bed all day. She and Tristan had been up most of the night discussing what might be behind the door. Ogres, witches, goblins, or maybe it was just people. One thing they both decided on was to write a letter. Just in case they got through the door but didn't know how to get out. That way, Aunt Betty could send out a search party for them. Gertrude placed it under her pillow. It would be easy to find, she thought.

Carmel mooed happily as Gertrude pulled on her udder. She sat on the milking stool with her eyes closed resting against Carmel's ample belly. What could be behind a door in a tree? She felt anxious about their planned trip for that afternoon. That was if Aunt Betty gave them the afternoon off.

'Are you alright?' asked Aunt Betty.

Gertrude slumped over her bowl of porridge. 'Oh, yes I am.' Quickly sitting upright in her chair and tapped Tristan on the leg to do the same.

'Hurry up with you then. It's about time for your English lesson. I have three new words for you to learn.

Gertrude and Tristan sauntered from the table and went into the sitting room. Gertrude loved English lessons the most, though today she was too tired to care. Tristan was already complaining. He much preferred mathematics; it made sense to him.

The morning crept by like a snail. The clock above the mantle seemed to tick louder than normal. Gertrude had to continually nudge Tristan. He had his head resting on his hand, and every now and again, he would close his eyes. Gertrude had to admit Aunt Betty was a fine teacher, and she was so glad to have the opportunity to learn. Most schools in Britania were closed because of the war. And here they were on a farm safe and sound getting an education. Gertrude thought about the letter she and Tristan had written last night.

Dear Aunt Betty, If Tristan and I don't return home this afternoon we've been gobbled up by the door in the woods. Please rescue us. I have memorised how to get there. From Carmel's shed from the corner where the sun hits it in the afternoon walk straight as possible through the two fields and keep walking till you come to the Woods. Then turn left and walk 334 steps to the right. Not big steps or you'll miss the opening into the woods. You'll know it's the exact spot when you see an old fence post. Now follow the white looking stones until you see a large tree wrapped with a vine hanging almost to the floor of the Woods. There should be a boulder to the left. If you find the right place pull the vines away and you will find a door.

'Gertrude, Gertrude,' Aunt Betty was calling.

Gertrude came out of her daze.

'Right, you two, what on earth is going on?' Gertrude and Tristan looked at each other as if to say;

keep the door in the woods a secret.

'We are just a bit tired, that's all,' said Gertrude.

'It was the wind last night. I didn't sleep well,' Tristan blurted out.

'Me too,' said Gertrude grimacing.

'The wind? I sleep like a baby. I didn't hear the wind, but I heard someone up.'

'My throat was a bit dry; I had some milk and honey,' said Gertrude. Clearing her throat to emphasise.

'Well, that's it for lessons today. I doubt that anything I have taught you now, would sink in.' Aunt Betty turned to her writing desk and pulled a few envelopes out. Tristan winked at Gertrude just before Aunt Betty turned back around. Now they could go down to the woods earlier than expected.

'Can we go and get some fresh air and walk through the fields?' questioned Gertrude.

'We can check the fences at the same time to see if any of them need fixing,' suggested Tristan.

'What a great idea. Then home for lunch on the first bell and an afternoon nap.'

'Well, that didn't work, did it,' said Tristan when they were far enough away from the house.

'No. But we'll get our chance. Anyway, we're both too tired to be chased by goblins,' she said, smiling at her own joke.

'Stop it.'

For the next hour, they surveyed the fences and came back to report that only one fence on the far side of the barn needed mending.

Chapter 10

'Come on, Gert,' Tristan yelled as he ran up the driveway.

Well, he didn't have to wear a dress to church, Gertrude thought as she increased her pace. They had stopped at the mailbox at the end of the driveway and decided to walk until Tristan turned it into a race. They both burst through the kitchen door one after the other.

Aunt Betty was laying the table for lunch. 'Why are you two in such a hurry?'

'It's a race,' Tristan blurted out.

'Well, lad, it looks like you won. I have your favourite, beef pie with mash.'

'Yum,' they sang in unison.

Tristan and Gertrude had been plotting a

discussion with Aunt Betty before Tristan raced off. They had decided to give Aunt Betty some indication as to what direction they would be heading that afternoon.

'Aunt Betty. Tristan and I have decided to go exploring together today. We are heading straight passed the barn and walking towards the woods. I found a wonderful spot for a picnic last time I went down that way. Can we take a drink, and a scone each to have while we are there?'

'That sounds like a marvelous idea. I should come with you?'

'Oh um, we want to tidy it up a bit first. And besides, it's hard to walk through all that long grass,' said Gertrude.

'Righto. Get changed when you have finished here. Oh, and don't get lost.'

***

'That was easy,' Tristan said. They passed Carmel's barn and formed a straight line heading for the woods. A bunch of thunderous clouds had drifted across the sky. It was considerably darker when Gertrude and Tristan reached the opening of the woods. It looked like the dark tunnel of no return.

'Well, we are here now, let's do this,' said Gertrude, her voice sounding braver than she felt. She could feel the food loosen in her stomach.

Don't be sick now.

She grabbed Tristan's hand as they delved deeper into the woods. The stones were still visible. She wondered why no one had ever found the door before. And she also wondered whether it was a good idea to leave the stones there. She didn't want to share their discovery, not yet. Maybe not at all.

'Look, the door. It's open,' said Tristan pulling the vines away to reveal the slightly ajar door. Gertrude edged closer, stretched her neck, and peeked around the door. All the while, her heart was racing like a motor car.

'Can you see any strange creatures?' Tristan asked in quite a loud whisper.

'Come on, this is what we are here for, to see what's behind the door.'

'Alright brave one, you go first. But what if we can't get out?' said Tristan.

'I left the letter for Aunt Betty. Let's just hope she finds it if we don't return.'

They pushed the door open wide enough to shuffle through. Arms linked, they tentatively slipped inside. On either side of the door was a long stone wall that went further than Gertrude could see.

'Shh look,' she said, putting her hand over Tristan's mouth, pointing to the little man with pointy ears sitting under a tree.

But just as Gertrude spoke something weird began to happen. They watched each other in horror. Their bodies started to bulge and deflate, first one arm than a leg. Gertrude's head blew up as big as a watermelon. Then went down to the size of a large potato.

'Aunty Betty isn't going to like this,' said Tristan.

'This is hardly the time to joke. What are we going to do?'

But with all the commotion they hadn't noticed the door was barred. The little man with pointy ears now stood next to them. He was hiccupping.

'What has happened to us?' said Gertrude prodding and pinching herself thinking she was dreaming. She looked back at the door. It was way taller than her. How would they get out if they can't reach the doorknob?

'Who are you?' said Tristan getting straight to the point. The little man – well not so little anymore now they had shrunk to his size couldn't answer Tristan straight away. He just kept hiccupping.

'Hiccup. Who goes there?' he finally said.

'We um…the door, it was open sir,' answered Gertrude in an ever so polite voice.

'Hiccup. Who goes there?' he repeated.

'Oh, good afternoon, this is Tristan,' she said, waving her hand towards him. 'And I'm Gertrude. We live on a farm not far from here.'

'You're up and about early.'

Gertrude and Tristan looked at each other confused.

Tristan looked down at his watch and shook his head; not really sure what the little man meant. By his watch it was close to 2 o'clock in the afternoon.

'I am Gilmyer, the Keeper of the Gate,' he said in a surprisingly deep voice for a small person.

'Why are you hiccupping?' Gertrude asked while she was trying to make sense of her surroundings.

A real elf. How exciting.

'Oh, I must have drunk too much bubble and pop. You're a silly elf. You're supposed to be watching the gate,' he ranted to himself.

'I know a cure for the hiccups,' said Gertrude. 'Hold your nose and take a deep breath. Now count to ten slowly.'

Gilmyer followed her instruction. His face started to go a deep red, but when he took some air into his lungs, the hiccups had stopped.

'Thanks, Missy.'

'How do we get back to our normal size?' asked Tristan, still poking and prodding himself, and Gertrude.

'Stop it,' she said.

'Um. Oh yes, that's right. When you go back through the gate.'

'Oh, just as well. I don't think Aunt Betty would like us to stay this size,' replied Tristan.

'Where are we, Gilmyer?' asked Gertrude as she tapped Tristan on the shoulder to look at the distant village she could see.

'Welcome to Hollow Woods,' said Gilmyer. Then he blew a whistle that pierced the still air.

Chapter 11

Several elves armed with bows and arrows surrounded Gertrude and Tristan. They looked back at Gilmyer. But he had taken his position back under the shade of the tree to guard the gate.

'I didn't see that coming,' said Tristan. They huddled together hand in hand. 'This is becoming a habit,' he joked.

Gertrude rolled her eyes and moved in the direction the army of elves were pushing them. They walked through a narrow tree-lined path. It opened up into what looked like a small village. It wasn't your typical Britania countryside village. The first building they passed was made of mud bricks. The roof was thatched with plaited leaves and there were many shades of tulips sitting in buckets outside one of the buildings. A pretty girl sat on a wooden bench beside them.

'I demand to see your leader,' Gertrude announced. But nobody took any notice.

'We must escape, Tristan. Aunt Betty will worry if we don't make it home before dark.'

'Well, what's your plan, genius? Oh, too late,' he said as they stopped abruptly. One of the elves blew a horn and looked up at a cage attached to a rope as it made its way to the ground.

'Get in,' a guard said.

Gertrude and Tristan stood their ground.

'I'm not going up there.' Gertrude folded her arms and straightened. Planting her feet. But the guard was strong and soon shoved them into the cage.

'But…I need to get home,' shouted Gertrude as the ground got further and further away. She began to cry.

Tristan pulled her close and hugged her. 'We'll be alright. They don't look that mean.' He wasn't sure if he was trying to convince himself or Gertrude.

Gertrude and Tristan screamed as the cage came

to an abrupt stop. They were high up in the biggest tree Gertrude had ever seen. Though it wasn't big at all if she was her normal size. They were dragged out of the cage by another guard waiting at the top. Gertrude dried her eyes on the sleeve of her shirt. She noticed a man sitting on a throne. That must be the leader, she thought.

I must be dreaming. She pinched herself and Tristan.

'What was that for?'

'Just checking.' Her legs were starting to feel like jelly.

Tristan was rubbing his hand together as if he was trying to start a fire. That was what he did when he got nervous.

They were frightened. What would happen next? Would they return to the farm? Or would the elves take them prisoner?

To Gertrude, it felt like everything was in slow motion. They stood at attention a few steps away from the man on the throne. Now closer, Gertrude thought he looked kind. She wiped her eyes and nose again, trying to compose herself.

His hair was jet black with strands of grey mixed through. It was drawn back into a braid hanging over his shoulder and hung down to his waist. His skin was well-tanned and muscular.

'I am Mortar, the leader of Hollow Woods. What is your business here?' he boomed.

Gertrude cleared her throat. 'Please, sir, we don't mean any harm. I am Gertrude, and this is Tristan.'

'I don't need to know your names. Why are you here?'

'Sir um…the door was open and well… we wanted to know what was inside,' replied Tristan.

'Please, sir,' begged Gertrude. We need to get home before dark. We promise we won't tell anyone about Hollow Woods.'

'How can I trust two strangers?'

'But…'

At that moment, a young elf walked straight up to Mortar and bowed. It was the same girl Gertrude had seen on the way to the village. She was beautiful. She had braided buttercup blonde hair, a slender waist, and eyes blue like the ocean circled with thick lashes.

Gertrude had to nudge Tristan to stop him from staring.

'Chief, look at them. Can't you see they are just children? They can't harm us.'

'Now, Summer, I know you mean well,' he said, in a much softer tone. 'But we haven't had invaders for centuries.'

'I know. But they are hardly invaders. Just curious like any child would be. We could learn from them. Find out what is happening out there in the human world? It could be important to our defence,' she finally said smiling and winking at Gertrude.

Gertrude tried to smile but she was worried that a) they would be captured never to return, or b) they finally escaped only to find Aunt Betty had grounded them for life. Neither scenario ended well.

Mortar scratched his head while he looked at Gertrude and Tristan. They stood ever so still huddled close to each other.

'How old are you?' he asked leaning closer, his deep brown eyes burning into them.

'We are only twelve years old. Please sir…chief, we

need to go home,' Gertrude begged. Daringly she stepped closer as new tears spilled down her face.

'Alright, alright. Enough. I will let you go. But you must return the day after your next full moon,' Mortar said, in a much kinder voice. 'The Council of the Four Lands will meet and decide your destiny, and whether you are permitted entry to Hollow Woods for us to study and learn from you.'

'You're not going to chop us up into little pieces to study us, are you?' asked Tristan.

'Of, course not, boy.'

'Alright.' Gertrude nodded in agreement. 'But who are…The Council of the Four Lands?'

'It comprises of the leaders of the Dwarves, Goblins, and Trolls,' said Summer.

'Wow, and double wow.' said Tristan.

'Now leave before I change my mind.' He shooed them away with his hand.

But Tristan stopped in his tracks feeling braver. 'So, you won't kill us when we return, will you?'

Mortar's smirk turned into a grin. 'You have my word, young man. I won't kill you.

'I'll escort them to the door,' said Summer, excitement in her voice.

'Thank you for helping us. I don't know what Mortar might have done if you didn't stick up for us,' said Gertrude.

'Oh him. His voice might be scary, but he has a gentle soul.' Summer led them back along the trail towards the door.

'Look, we're here. When you arrive, next time make three quick raps on the door and Gilmyer will let you in.'

Gilmyer nodded at them and unlatched the oversized door with a large pole.

'Thank you,' they said. Gertrude and Tristan walked through the door, and as they did, they changed back to their normal size.

'Thank goddess for that,' said Tristan, checking all his body parts were intact.

Gertrude took in a deep breath and felt reassured that they made it out alive. She thought when they were captured in a strange land that there would be no way her parents would ever find her.

'It's still light out here,' said Tristan as they emerged out from the tree canopy. 'It felt like we had been gone for ages. The sun was fading in Hollow Woods before we left. Strange.'

'You're right. I wonder what it means?'

***

'Back so soon,' said Aunt Betty as they piled through the kitchen door.

'But I thought it was…,' said Tristan.

'Thought it was what, dear?'

'Never mind.'

Gertrude gave Tristan a look and nodded towards the bedroom. 'We might go and read for a while,' she said dragging Tristan behind her.

'Goodo, I'll just have a little nap.'

They sat on the floor in the middle of Tristan's room, deep in thought.

'Why is it still early afternoon here and close to sundown there,' Tristan said, pointing out the window.

'Shh, we don't want Aunt Betty hearing us.

'Well, why?'

'How would I know? Let me think.' Gertrude got up and started pacing from the door to the window; she could think better on her feet.

'Have you finished thinking yet?'

'Does that mean that time passes at a slower rate out here than in Hollow Woods?' she finally said. Plonking down on the floor next to Tristan, contemplating her own question. 'What's the time?' she said tapping on Tristan's watch.

Tristan looked down at his watch then put it close to his ear.

'It seems to have stopped.'

'Great,' Gertrude drew in a deep breath. What Gertrude was thinking was that when they next visited Hollow Woods, they would be able to stay longer?

***

'Come on, you two,' Aunt Betty opened Tristan's bedroom door. 'You've been in here for hours.'

They followed Aunty Betty to the kitchen, sat at the table and waited for the delicious-smelling stew to be served up.

'When is the next full moon?' Tristan asked in between mouthfuls.

'I'm not sure, love. But Mr. James might know,' said Aunt Betty.

'Well, how often is there a full moon?'

'Still don't know…but if you look out the window each night you will soon find out.'

Tristan rose from the table, pulled the lace curtains apart, and stared up into the night sky. 'Nothing but stars.'

Chapter 12

Mr. James spent a lot of time helping on the farm. The very next day after their lessons Tristan helped move some hay and clean out Carmel's stall. It was the job he hated most; it stunk. Tristan couldn't hold his nose at the same time as he shovelled. The manure was used in the garden that surrounds the house. Gertrude and Aunt Betty had been working hard to turn what used to be weeds and grass into a lush cottage garden.

Tristan had tied a large handkerchief around his face to curb the smell. And each time the shovel hit the manure the stench would invade his nostrils.

When he was first introduced to this chore he ran from the barn and begged Aunt Betty to send him back to the orphanage. She had laughed and marched him back out to the barn herself and shovelled the cow poo with him. Nothing was wasted on the farm; Aunt Betty made sure of it. Even the eggshells were reused for plant fertilizer.

'Mr. James, when is the next full moon?'

'Well, I'm not exactly sure. But I did notice it was a half-moon last night.'

'But I looked out of the kitchen window, and I couldn't see it.'

'Well son, that's because the moon orbits the earth. So, you were looking out the wrong window. What's your interest in the moon?

'Oh, um…well, I don't know. I was just wondering about it,' said Tristan trying to make out that it was no big deal.

'Check with Aunt Betty and if she doesn't mind, I can take you to the library in town tomorrow after your lessons.'

'Oh, thank you, Mr. James.'

***

'Look what I got at the library,' Tristan said pushing the front door open. Gertrude looked up from the book she was reading and marked her place. She followed Tristan into his room, shutting the door behind them.

'The librarian said these are the best books for our age and that the full moon isn't too far away. Here you look through this one,' he said. He handed Gertrude one of the books. They sat on the large oval mat in the middle of the room reading and making notes.

'Look, Tristan. I think I've found it. Mr. James told you that it was a half-moon two nights ago. Well, listen to this. It takes about a month for the moon to orbit the earth and go through all the phases. Wait a minute,' she said, skimming further down the page. 'Here is it. Halfway through the phases it's called waning, in about the third week. That's when it becomes the full moon. You can tell because when you look at the moon, the sun is in the opposite direction.

'But you can't see the sun at night.'

'Yes, but you can sometimes see the moon during the day.'

'So, by what you're saying, we have less than a week to go?'

***

It was the day after the full moon and the weekend, perfect. Gertrude milked Carmel as quickly as anyone could milk a cow and ran into the kitchen for breakfast. Aunt Betty was by the stove stirring a pot of porridge. Tristan was sitting at the table in the middle of the room staring at his watch that Mr. James had given him so he wouldn't be late doing his chores. His still wasn't working.

'Your breakfast is almost ready, my dears.' Aunt Betty turned the stove off, tugged at the tea towel that hung beside the stove, and carried the hot saucepan to the table. Gertrude and Tristan sat straighter in their chairs. They were eager to set off on their adventure. They didn't even wait for Aunt Betty to be seated before they ploughed into their breakfast.

'Well, you two seem to be in a hurry today.' She gave them a stern look with a tinge of a smile.

'Oh. Um, not really' blurted Tristan.

Then Gertrude said calmly, 'We have decided to

go on a picnic near the edge of the woods.'

'That sounds lovely, my dear. Would you like me to pack you some food?'

'Yes, please.'

'I'll come with you.'

Gertrude and Tristan looked at each other as if to say, what do we do now? They had already put Aunt Betty off once. Neither of them wanted to hurt her feelings; she was so nice to them.

It was mid-morning before they all set off for their picnic. They walked in single file. Past Carmel's barn and through the fields of long grass. Gertrude was conjuring up a plan to send Aunt Betty back to the farm. There were so many ideas whirling around in her head. But she had to pick only one idea otherwise Aunt Betty could become suspicious.

The grass will ruin your hem. Mr. James was calling by. You'll get too puffed out. I forgot to let Carmel out. The eggs will go off in the sun. Ah ha, the scones are still in the oven.

Gertrude stopped abruptly causing Tristan and Aunt Betty to almost fall into a pile.

'What on earth have you stopped for?' asked Aunt

Betty.

'Oh, the scones. Did you get the scones out of the oven?'

'Yes, my dear, it was clever of you to think of that. I wrapped a few scones before we left to bring with us. They should be still nice and warm by the time we reach the other side of the field.'

That didn't work. Gertrude shrugged her shoulders at Tristan and continued on the path. It was a lovely sunny day. Once they reached the clearing Aunt Betty spread an old blanket on the slightly dewy grass for them to rest on.

From where they sat, Gertrude could see the opening to the woods. She wanted to draw Aunt Betty attention away from the woods, so she said, 'Tristan did you bring your fishing rod?'

'No,' he said, sounding a bit confused.

'Oh, never mind. Have you been down to the brook over yonder?' she asked Aunt Betty. Gertrude pointing in the opposite direction of woods.

'Why yes, dear. Mr. Appleton and I would come down here when we were courting. He proposed to me right under the shade of that tree over there.' She pointed to a grand old tree close to the bank of the brook. 'I wish he had met both of you,' she said with a sigh.

While Tristan and Gertrude explored the brook Aunt Betty sat happily on the blanket watching them. She looked like she was enjoying the day and Gertrude felt guilty for trying to send her home. They decided they may as well have fun as they wouldn't be visiting Hollow Woods today. Though Gertrude was concerned that if they didn't return when they were told to, Mortar would forbid them entry to Hollow Woods. Gertrude didn't want that to happen. She wanted to see Summer. And most of all she wanted to learn more about Hollow Woods and the Council of the Four Lands.

The brook was running slow, a trickle really. Tristan kicked off his shoes and waded in the fresh, clear water. He used his hands trying to catch the tiny fish swimming upstream. But just when he thought he had one they would slip through his fingers.

Gertrude laughed at him each time. She sat under

the shade of a tree. She picked wildflowers splitting a hole in the stem like the eye of a needle. Then she threaded the flower to the next one, until it was long enough to sit on her head like a crown.

Gertrude looked up to she Aunt Betty waving frantically to get their attention. She motioned to Tristan, and they ran to Aunt Betty; worried something was wrong. Aunt Betty looked like she was doing a dance when they reached her.

'What's wrong, asked Gertrude.

'I'll leave you two here. I must head back now. Nature calls.'

'Oh,' said Gertrude, raising her eyes at Tristan, a smile growing on her face.

'Be back before dark, my dears,' Aunt Betty yelled over her shoulder as she waddled her way back to the house.

Chapter 13

'Right. Tristan. You watch, and make sure Aunt Betty can't see us, while I pack up the picnic stuff.'

'So, if I can't see Aunt Betty anymore, she shouldn't be able to see me?' Gertrude tip-toed looking over the long grass before she answered Tristan.

'Yes, it's safe now. Let's go.'

They raced to the entrance of the woods and ended up bent over gulping in air. It was almost midday. The woods weren't as dark as before but still looked scary. Gertrude caught hold of Tristan's hand at the first noise she heard.

'I know I'm irresistible,' he said.

'Don't be stupid, Tristan,' she said, pulling her

hand from his.

'Sorry,' he said as he grabbed her hand at the next noise.

It wasn't long before they found the door again. Gertrude was about to knock.

'Do you remember the secret knock?

Gertrude rolled her eyes. 'Of course, I do.'

'Well, what is it?

'Three quick knocks like this.' She rapped on the door. They stood waiting for permission to entry Hollow Woods. They didn't know what to expect. They were greeted at the door by Gilmyer and Summer. Gertrude smiled. She already liked Summer. She didn't miss the orphanage, but she missed talking to her friends. Summer was much older than Gertrude, in her twenties Gertrude guessed.

Having Summer there to greet them gave her hope that there would be plenty more visits to Hollow Woods.

They walked through the door and as they did that strange sensation hit them again. They watched each other shrink again.

'Wow, that feels so strange,' said Tristan.

'You do look rather funny,' said Summer. 'Come on, The Council of The Four Lands is waiting in the Great Hall.

The Great Hall was through a large hollow underneath the tree where Gertrude and Tristan had first met Mortar. The roots of the tree made up the roof and the walls with long well-lit tunnels leading off from each side. The ground that should have been dirt was decorated with off-white marble tiles with a round symbol in the middle of the floor.

'Why is this tree so big?' asked Gertrude, taking in the enormity of it. The Great Hall was crowded with many elves and a few strange-looking creatures.

'This tree "Shandalar" is what keeps the Four Lands safe. It is sacred to us. It tells us when the new season is coming. There are a few among us who can talk with her.

'But it's just a tree? And how do you know it's a she?' asked Tristan.

'You'll see,' was Summer's response.

Summer led Tristan and Gertrude to the main

table where the leaders of The Four Lands sat. Mortar was one of the leaders and three other strange creatures. She bowed and shuffled back into the crowd leaving Gertrude and Tristan standing in front of the group of four.

A bell chimed. The crowd moved closer around Gertrude and Tristan. Mortar raised his hand, and as he did, the elves too, acknowledge their leader. The room became silent. All attention was on Mortar.

'My fellow folks of Hollow Woods, The Council of the Four Lands has assembles today to decide the fate of these two children.'

Tristan gulped. Gertrude took his hand. She felt like she was on trial. She was looking at the creatures sitting beside Mortar for any sign of acceptance. The closest to a human face was the smallest creature that looked like a dwarf.

'Let me introduce and acknowledge Rakash, leader of the Trolls, Bostrabelle leader of the dwarfs, and Zrork, leader of the Goblins. Be well, my fellow Councillors.

Rakash, the leader of the Trolls, was first to speak.

'I lost most of my clan in the Great Battle with the humans. I vote for the safety of my people. I vote, no.

'Gees, we are only twelve years old,' whispered Tristan through the side of his mouth. 'What could we do to destroy this place?' Gertrude gave him a stern look but understood his reasoning.

'Bostrabelle, please give us your vote,' asked Mortar. The dwarf stood on a box that sat just underfoot. When the dwarf spoke, Gertrude realised the dwarf was female.

'I would like to welcome these children. Living in harmony is not always sort by the clans of The Four Land.' She looked at the Troll leader, Rakash, as she said this. 'My vote is yes.' There was a rumble of voices in the crowd.

Mortar raised his hand again to gain silence in the room. 'We will now hear from the Goblin leader, Zrork.

Gertrude couldn't believe that by coming through a wooden door in a tree that they had discovered not just the elves, but also dwarfs, trolls and goblins. She thought even if she told anyone about Hollow

Woods, they would never believe her.

Zrork leaned in towards the crowd. The words from his mouth were foreign to Tristan and Gertrude. When he finished speaking the room erupted with cheers. Gertrude tried to look back into the crowd to find Summer. She felt Summer wanted them to stay. But she couldn't see her. Gertrude looked back at Tristan and then to Mortar.

What had happened?

Mortar rose from his Throne. 'We are making history today. Not for three hundred years have we allowed humans back into our treasured lands. This is a test of friendship. And through this friendship we will gain great knowledge. This knowledge can be passed down to future clans. Let us welcome Gertrude and Tristan.'

Gertrude and Tristan hugged. From behind them Summer appeared with a few other elf girls and took Gertrude by the arm and led her down to the most beautiful fields filled with rows and rows of tulips.

Tristan was greeted by Logan who introduced himself as Mortar's son. Tristan showed his gratitude by continually calling him Your Highness. They marched off toward the woodlands inside Hollow Woods. A shooting range had been setup. Logan handed Tristan a bow and arrow.

'Here, aim for that target.'

***

'Why do you grow so many tulips,' Gertrude asked.

'The tulips are a gift to Shandalar, our mother tree. Without her, we would not survive. The tulips are an offering to bring in the most important season of all. Spring, the season of growth. You must come to the festival; it's on the next high sun. It's so much fun.'

Summer got Gertrude straight to work picking the tulips. Summer's friends, Jasmin, and Lily, worked alongside them. The four girls gathered armfuls of tulips in an array of pinks, reds, yellows, and mauves. The flowers were then placed in large squatted barrells of water to keep them fresh for the dawning day.

'I'll try,' said Gertrude. 'But it's Sunday tomorrow. Aunt Betty expects us to go to church in the morning,' She could see by the frown on Summer's face that she was a bit confused.

"What is the meaning of Sunday and morning?' questioned Summer adding a bit more water to the barrells.

'Well, the morning is when the sun first comes up and the sky becomes light. Sunday is what we call one of those days. There are seven days in a week all with a different name. It helps keeps track of time.'

'Oh, we are guided by nature. The moon, the stars, the sun, and the whispers on the wind. Look at the Sun; it is getting close to Yawning. Gertrude looked up at the sky and noticed the sun was setting. *That makes sense.*

'We must head home before the sun sets,' said Gertrude, hoping that was easier for Summer to understand.

'See you on the next High Sun,' Summer called out. Gertrude found Tristan and they headed home. Both were reluctant to leave, but excited about their next visit.

Chapter 14

'Do we have to go to church today?' asked Tristan. Aunt Betty spat on her hand and slid it through Tristan's hair, trying to keep his unruly locks of hair in place.

'You need a haircut, my boy. Come on you two. Mr. James will be here shortly,' Aunt Betty ignored Tristan's question, which was repeated each Sunday.

Gertrude didn't mind going to church; it was the one thing that Aunt Betty demanded from them. And if Aunt Betty was happy, she was more likely to allow them to roam that afternoon.

'Tristan and I have decided to go fishing this afternoon.' Gertrude blurted out as they walked through the double doors of the church.

'Alright, dear. I'll give you my decision after lunch.' Aunt Betty regularly played that game. She would always let them have fun. Except for that one time when Tristan had spilled a whole bucket of Carmel's milk because he insisted on carrying it for Gertrude.

It was after 12 o'clock when they finally returned home. Gertrude was itching to get over to Hollow Woods and see her new friends. Lunch was on the stove and just needed heating up. Gertrude and Tristan gobbled up the delicious pea and potato soup mopping up what was left with a fist-size knob of bread.

"My goodness, I didn't realise you were that hungry. Would you like some more?'

'No thanks,' they chorused.

'May we go fishing now,' asked Tristan. They stood and tucked in their chairs.

'Of course, you can,' said Aunt Betty in between mouthfuls of soup. They turned to make their exit through the back door.

'Um, my dears, have you forgotten something?' They looked at each other, not sure of what she meant. And then Gertrude went over and planted a kiss on Aunt Betty's cheek followed by Tristan.

'No, that's not what I meant. Weren't you going fishing?'

'Oh yes,' said Tristan nudging Gertrude to follow him.

A few minutes later they were armed with their fishing gear and marched out the door. They hid the fishing rods in the long grass just past Carmel's barn and ran all the way to the entrance of the woods. They didn't have long this time, about four hours. But how would they know when to go back? The time in Hollow Woods seemed to go faster than out in the real world.

Gertrude was trying to make sense of it as Tristan rapped on the door. Gilmyer opened the wooden door.

'Well, hello Gilmyer,' said Tristan walking through the door with Gertrude behind him. Gilmyer bolted the door shut behind them. This time they were not afraid of what lay ahead. They stood still while their bodies were reduced to the size of an elf. It was hilarious to watch. Their bodies would form many different shapes. Like when a balloon is half-empty, and the air was pushed around to make funny shapes. Another thing that amazed Gertrude is how their clothes shrink with them. What other magic lived here?

'Has the Tulip Festival begun?' asked Gertrude as they made their way up the path towards a crowd of elves.

'You're just in time for the grand finale,' exclaimed Gilmyer.

'Wonderful, let's hurry.' Gertrude caught Tristan's hand and sprinted up the narrow track.

There was a large gathering in the courtyard in front of the Great Hall. A group of young elves stood near the entrance to the hall, all holding a bunch of tulips. Gilmyer had finally caught up to them. Panting, half-bent with his hands on knees, trying to suck air back into his lungs.

'What are they doing, Gilmyer?' asked Tristan standing on his tiptoes to see over the mass of elves in front of him.

'Oh, we are about to vote for the next Miss Tulip.'

'Look, there's Summer,' Tristan pointed out. Summer stood in a line of six female elves. They all donned a ring of daisies on their heads and smiled nervously back at the crowd. Summer's long blonde hair had been wound up, braided, and piled on the top of her head; it looked like a crown. In comparison, Gertrude's unruly red locks hung to her shoulders.

'So how do you decide on a winner?' asked Gertrude, also balancing on her toes to get a better look.

'It's easy, really. We just clap and whistle and the loudest wins,' said Gilmyer. I'm voting for Lily this year.' His face turned scarlet. Each elf on stage stepped forward, said a few words, stated their intention, and swore to uphold their duty of being Miss Tulip, then the voting began. Gertrude and Tristan joined in on the voting. Jasmin received the loudest claps and whistles and was voted as Miss Tulip.

At the end of the crowning ceremony all the

contestants threw their tulips into the crowd. Gertrude could see Summer squeezing through the crowd making her way towards them. She must have spotted them earlier.

'Hi, Gertrude and Tristan, come with me. I want you to meet someone.' Summer grabbed them both by the hand. They snaked back through the crowd towards a path which lead to the tulips field. A group of mudbrick huts with roofs of braided reeds stood in a small clearing. One of the huts was surrounded by a mass of colour. Barrels of tulips sat on a wooden bench under a carved out open window. A handsome young elf stood to the left of the barrels. His large brown eyes widened with delight as they approached. He had a bow and arrow slung on his back.

'This is Logan, son of Mortar.'

'Oh, it's a pleasure to see you again, holy one,' said Tristan. He bowed at the waist. Both Summer and Logan burst into laughter followed by Gertrude and Tristan.

'There's no need to bow, Tristan,' said Logan in a deep smooth voice, similar to his father's. 'And this must be Gertrude.' He smiled.

'Hello, Logan.' She offering her hand to shake. Both Logan and Summer looked puzzled at the gesture.

'Oh, you don't know what I'm offering.'

'No, sorry, Gertrude.'

Tristan butted in, grabbed Gertrude's hand, and shook it. 'See.'

'Tristan is trying to demonstrate the way we formally greet each other.'

'Oh,' said Logan, stretching out his hand for Gertrude to shake.

'We are so lucky to have humans among us again. We can learn so much from you,' said Logan.

'What is your way of greeting?' asked Gertrude.

'Oh, we acknowledge each other in a far deeper way. It is a gift we are born with; some with insights that help protect our people. We greet with our mind and soul,' said Logan.

'Wow, that's deep,' said Tristan. And once again they all buckled in laughter.

'I understand you have been learning the skill of

arrow shooting. Tristan,' said Summer.

Tristan nodded in answer.

'Yes, after only one practice I can see he has a steady hand and a keen eye. He will make a worthy marksman one day,' said Logan.

'I will?'

'Yes, Tristan, you shall. Come, it is time for your next lesson.'

Summer led Gertrude into her home. There were long leaf straps sitting on a plaited mat and a stack of woven cane baskets stood in one corner leaning against the mud wall. Summer sat on the mat and Gertrude followed.

'I'll show you how to make a basket.' Summer picked up three pieces of the long leaf straps and woven them together in a braid. She kept doing this until she had enough to commence working on a basket.

Gertrude watched for a while then Summer helped her to start a basket of her own. They sat together all afternoon until Gertrude saw the light dimming in the sky and knew it was time to head home.

'Thank you, Summer for showing me how to make a basket, but I have to go.' Gertrude stood and placed her newly made basket onto of the pile in the corner.

Summer followed her out of the hut. 'If you follow that path, you will find Logan and Tristan in the Woodlands.'

'See you next time,' said Gertrude giving Summer a hug.

'Till next time,' said Summer.

Gertrude walked down the path towards the Woodlands. She felt happier than she had for a long time. But feeling happy also brought with it a feeling of guilt. How could she be happy when she didn't know whether her parents were alive or dead? She called out to Tristan. She could see him through the trees. 'Tristan, it's time to go.'

'Did you see that,' he said as he raced up to Gertrude. 'I almost got a bullseye.'

'Yes, it looks like you're getting the knack of it. We better go.'

'Look at the sun, Tristan. It seems like it hasn't

moved at all,' said Gertrude squinting as they emerged from the shelter of the trees.

'That's strange.'

'Maybe Summer or Logan have the answer. We must ask them next time. Come on, I'll race you.'

Chapter 15

'I think we should stay longer this time,' said Tristan. It was Tuesday afternoon, only a few days after their last visit to Hollow Woods. And over that time, they had been debating whether time stood still in their world or whether it just went slower. Tristan's watch was fixed. And Tristan thought it had stopped working because they had entered Hollow Woods. After all, there was magic present there. How else would he and Gertrude shrink?

Gertrude suggested they leave the watch just outside the door when they entered Hollow Woods. That way, when the sun started to set in Hollow Woods, they could check the time. And know for sure if they had to return to the farm and Aunt Betty.

'Can you believe it, you and me once orphans, live

on a farm, and we get to visit elves through a door in a tree trunk?'

'It is truly unbelievable.'

Gertrude and Tristan were traipsing through the field on their way to Hollow Woods.

'I love archery. And I'm a natural, Logan told me.'

'I just hope you never have to use it on anything other than a target.' Gertrude pulled at the wire fence for them to squeeze through which was close to the entrance of woods.

'Oh, I couldn't shoot anyone.'

They met Gilmyer at the door and were escorted to the Great Hall to meet with Mortar.

'Have we done something wrong?' Gertrude questioned Gilmyer as they walked the narrow path which led into the village.

'I don't know. I was just asked to deliver you to our leader.'

Two elves Gertrude, recognised as the guards when they were captured, met Gilmyer halfway along the path.

'I'll take them from here,' one of them said.

Gertrude and Tristan looked questioningly back at Gilmyer, but he just shrugged.

Was Mortar going to banish them from Hollow Woods? Would he lock them up never to return to Aunt Betty? Gertrude thought back to their previous visit. They had watched the Tulip Festival, and she had sat with Summer all afternoon weaving a basket.

'What did you do, Tristan?' she said as they entered the Great Hall.

'Nothing, I swear. What did you do?' he retaliated. This made Gertrude worry even more.

Mortar was sitting on an oversized chair by a fireplace, his long lanky legs crossed. Gertrude watched his face trying to work out his mood.

He looks happy.

Gertrude and Tristan stood in front of Mortar. The guards left the room closing the thick wooden door behind them. Gertrude knew one thing. And that was as far as she knew, they had done everything expected of them so far. Surely Mortar was gaining trust in them.

Gertrude's brain ticked and her heart raced in

anticipation. Tristan was rubbing his hand together, his nervousness getting the better of him.

'You can't keep us prisoner, you know,' Gertrude blurted out. 'Aunt Betty will find us if we don't come home.'

'Dear child, I have no intention of making you and Tristan my prisoners,' Mortar said in a soft and soothing voice.

Gertrude and Tristan looked at each other and sighed.

'Oh, dear, we are so sorry, your Grace,' said Tristan as he bowed.

Gertrude clicked her tongue and shook her head as she pulled Tristan upright.

'I see you two have got the wrong impression as to why I summoned you. Let me explain,' Mortar said. He straightened up. 'Come, sit by the fire.'

Gertrude and Tristan sat cross-legged and waited for Mortar to continue. Though spring had just arrived there was still a slight chill.

'Many moons ago our world and your world lived in harmony. The people of Hollow Woods lived a simple life taking from the earth but always giving back to it. We have meagre possessions; we like it that way. My people started to become greedy with fights breaking out over silly things. At the time, the elders made the historical decision to protect our people and bring them back from disarray.'

'So is that why you were so worried when we first came to Hollow Woods,' Tristan said thoughtfully.

'Yes, young man. It is crucial to keep Hollow Woods a secret. We can't risk being exposed to the world out there. No one would understand our existence now.'

'I like it here, with fields of tulips, long rows of blueberry bushes, and Summer showed me how to make a basket out of leaves,' said Gertrude.

'I'm so pleased you enjoy your visits,' said Mortar with a smile on his face. 'I want your assurance that you will tell no one about The Four Lands and our citizens. And that everything you do will be for the good of Hollow Woods.

'We promise,' they chorused. Tristan crossed his heart with index finger.

'Who would believe us anyway?' added Tristan.

'I believe Logan is waiting for you, Tristan. He told me you are going well in the craft of archery. In fact, far beyond his expectation. He is well pleased with your progress.

'There is something I don't understand,' Tristan asked before he left. 'Why do you practice with a bow and arrows if you are peaceful people?' Gertrude elbowed Tristan in the ribs.

'Aww.'

'That's a reasonable question, young man. We intend to stay peaceful. But if ever we have intruders who mean to harm us, we will be prepared,' said Mortar. He rose from his chair. 'You can go now and find your friends, I just wanted to welcome you both and give you a bit of an understanding of how crucial it is to protect Hollow Woods.'

Tristan found Logan down among the trees in the practice zone. And Gertrude found Summer high up in a tree gathering bundles of branches filled with long leaves to renew the supply ready for the coming season.

'Come on up,' Summer yelled down to Gertrude. Gertrude stood beside Lily, who was gathering all the branches into different piles.

She craned her neck and yelled back. 'No, thank you, I'm quite happy down here.' Summer laughed. Lily nodded; she agreed with Gertrude. Summer easily climbed down the tree with the help of a few ropes and greeted Gertrude with a hug.

'I'm glad you came today. We're about to make floor rugs for our welcome to the Summer Festival.

'You certainly do have a lot of festivals,' Gertrude said.

'We welcome each season in. Each season provides us with different crops for us to survive,' said Summer in a more serious voice than usual.

'But you have just celebrated the coming in of spring.'

'Yes, but rugs take many a dawning to make.'

The three girls carried a pile of leaves back to Summer's hut. They sat on a circular mat in the middle of the room, stripping the leaves from the branches. The branches didn't go to waste. Logan and

Tristan arriving a while later to claim the branches worthy of making into arrows.

'Tristan and I have decided to stay longer. But we are confused about the time,' Gertrude started to explain. 'When we leave Hollow Woods, the sun seems to be in the same place as when we entered.'

'It would be nice if you could stay longer. I have never been out there in the human world. I'm not sure why your Sun hasn't moved. But what is time?'

'Oh, um. You tell the time of the day with the Dawning, High, and Yawning Sun. We use an object that straps to our wrist that counts each hour of the day.

'Why do you need to do that?'

Gertrude thought about how to answer that question. They lived by the stroke of the clock. Breakfast at seven in the morning, lunch at midday and supper at six o'clock. *Why do we do that?* She had never questioned it before now.

'I'm not sure. That's just what we do,' Gertrude answered honestly. 'When your Sun starts to yawn, Tristan and I will check his watch, the object that counts time.

We left it on the other side of the door.'

'What a great idea.'

Chapter 16

Gertrude had been sitting on the floor in the middle of Summer's hut for what seemed like hours. She was starting to get the knack of rugmaking. It was a simple process really. Braiding the leaves, joining them into long lengths with twine, and once long enough, snaking them around like a snail's shell and binding it all together.

Summer had told Gertrude that mat-making was shared amongst the elf clan. This season ten elves were working on the mats for the next season. Gertrude wondered why the rugs were made for the summer season and not the winter. But Summer told her that they are excellent at keeping the temperature down as the earth absorbs the heat. So, covering the floor made sense.

The noise of a horn, one long echo bellowed through Hollow Woods. 'Come on, Shandalar beckons,' said Summer.

'What?'

'You will see, my friend.' By the time they got to the courtyard where Shandalar stood, it was crowded. Everyone sat facing the giant tree and they were humming, rocking gently, side to side.

'A tree?' Gertrude had to admit it was a marvelous specimen, but she couldn't work out what species it was. She wondered if it would matter too much if she took one leaf back to Aunt Betty for inspection; she knew a lot about trees.

'What are they doing?' asked Gertrude, squeezing in close to Summer as she sat next to Lily and Jasmin.

'We are thanking Shandalar for life, for what she gives us. Each yawning of the sun we give thanks. We all hum until all the clan is here and we sing in our ancient tongue, our thanks. Then we share her offerings.'

Gertrude could see Tristan sitting next to Logan and waved. There was another long blow on the horn and the chanting began. It had a beautiful rhythm, the clan swaying in unison as they sang. It was very hypnotic, and Gertrude joined in trying to catch a few words. The volume rose and fell, the rhythm picked up speed, and then it happened.

The tree, Shandalar, began to sway to the chant. Her branches moved like the arms of a conductor swaying and catching specific beats in the song. Gertrude's mouth fell open. She looked at Summer, who nodded and smiled, still singing and swaying. Gertrude then looked at Tristan who had much the same reaction to her. It was so unreal, so fantastic to see. This was a moment she wished to savour. This was something that would intrigue her for a very long time.

Logan and Tristan joined Summer and Gertrude as they made their way into the Great Hall. There were rows of tables heavily laden with food.

'Where's the meat,' asked Tristan.

'Oh, we eat only what Shandalar provides us. Meat is taboo.'

Tristan looked a bit disappointed. They stepped in

line like everyone else and took a little from each bowl. Gertrude didn't recognise some of the dishes but that wasn't going to stop her from trying them. Mortar sat at a table facing out to the crowd. His plate piled high with food. He hadn't started eating yet. He smiled at Gertrude and Tristan as they made their way to a table close by. Logan excused himself and took a seat next to his father, with a vacant chair beside him.

'Who's supposed to sit next to Logan,' asked Tristan, leaning to speak to Lily.

'Oh, that is Baxter's seat. He very rarely chooses to share a feast with his clan.'

'Who is Baxter?' Gertrude asked this time.

'Logan's brother. He is entirely different from Logan. Not very friendly. He used to be once though. One day he just snapped. It happened not long after the death of his and Logan's mother.

Gertrude and Tristan exchanged glances.

'Well, it would be nice to meet him,' said Tristan taking a mouthful from the pile on his plate. 'This is delicious.'

'Tristan and I must check his watch to see what

time it is outside,' announced Gertrude after she finished the last forkful of food on her plate. She had been enjoying herself and had almost forgotten about it. She was surprised how full she was; having no meat didn't seem to matter.

'We will say goodbye now,' said Gertrude. 'Just in case we need to go back home.'

But just as they were about to leave Gilmyer racing into the Great Hall huffing and puffing. He whispered into Mortar's ear, who was nodding his understanding, his brow furrowed in a frown. Mortar raised his hand and the elf in the room raised their hands. Silence fell in the room.

'The door has been compromised. Return to your home and gather your loved ones.' Then Mortar signalled the horn blower. Three short sharp notes filled the area. Everyone grabbed hands and exited the hall.

'Follow me,' Summer said, grabbing Tristan's and Gertrude's hand.

'But we need to check the time,' Tristan said, as they raced to the safely of Summers' hut.

'You won't be going anywhere until the next high sun. We are in lockdown. You can stay with me for the night. It'll be fun,' Summer said, trying to smile.

Chapter 17

Mortar was in the Throne Room behind locked doors with guards on all exits. He sat at a long narrow table discussing the events with Gilmyer, who had raised the alarm. Bedside him sat Logan, and Mortar's trusted advisor, Tutu, the wise and ancient owl.

Tutu was perched on the back of a chair, his large round eye observing everyone in the room. Spectacles sat at the end of his beak.

Baxter burst into the room, coughing. 'So, the heir to the Throne finally shows his face,' said Mortar, trying to keep his anger in check.

'Father, a fire broke out at the West Side Armory. I didn't have time to raise the alarm, but I managed to put it out myself.'

'There seems to be a few things happening this

twilight,' stated Mortar, his mood softened slightly. Mortar was concerned that though he knew Gertrude and Tristan had nothing to do with these events, their presence in the community may have been the cause of the unrest. Or was someone using this time as an opportunity to avoid blame?

'Did you see anything out of the ordinary,' Tutu asked Gilmyer, who sat opposite his leader while Baxter took a seat beside him.

'No, not really. I saw a shape, a shadow, it was a lot taller than me. But it was on Twilight.'

'What? Like the height of a troll,' suggested Baxter.

'No, I don't know,' Gilmyer answered.

Mortar pondered the conversation for a while. He knew from experience that laying blame too early could begin an unnecessary war. And that was something he would prevent with much vigour. He was concerned for Baxter particularly. Mortar had witnessed Baxter's change in emotional state when his mother had been killed by the humans. And his decision to let Tristan and Gertrude into the elven community weighed heavily on him now. He had seen a change in Baxter's already rebellious character.

Mortar summoned his patrol leader to call on more volunteers to check the Door, and the West Side Armory. And to check all the gates to the other Lands had not been tampered with.

'Did you see anything while you were so conveniently near the Armory?' asked Logan, doubting his brother's bravery. Baxter always told them what he did, though no one ever saw him in action.

Baxter stood. His chair crashed to the floor as he rounded the table.

'Sit,' commanded Mortar. Baxter stopped dead in his tracks and stared at Logan, his eyes reduced to thin slits. Taking a deep loud breath, Baxter restrained himself.

'Sit,' Mortar repeated.

Baxter dragged himself back to his seat.

'Did you see anything?' ask Mortar.

'Yes, Father, I believe I did. Like Gilmyer, I believe this is the work of the Trolls. They voted against allowing the humans access to our sacred lands, as would have I. You must banish them, Father.'

'Hush now, Baxter. They are children; they have no malice in them, just curiosity. I understand your reluctance, but can't you see this is different? There is no more to be said. Thank you for your brave efforts in dousing the fire.'

'I never said it was the Trolls,' Gilmyer fired back at Baxter after he allowed the leader to finish talking.

Baxter just shrugged.

'There is nothing any of you can do. Leave now while I discuss the events with Tutu. Once the room was clear, Mortar slouched in his chair.

Tutu jumped from the back of the chair onto the table facing Mortar. 'What do you feel is the best way forward, Master?'

'I feel a war brewing. But I can't say it's with the Trolls. But the Trolls do seem to be the likely instigators.'

'It doesn't make sense though. The gates are barred and locked to The Tower of Zebajin.'

Mortar looked at his friend for a moment before

answering. 'Have we a traitor among us?' he said, more to himself than to Tutu. 'We must call a special meeting of the Four Lands.'

Chapter 18

'See you, Gilmyer,' Tristan said. He and Gertrude watched him shut the wooden door behind them.

'Grab your watch and let's hurry. We need to know what time it is,' said Gertrude.

Tristan searched the spot where he had left his watch, but it wasn't there.

'It's gone. That's strange.'

Gertrude checked in the same place. 'Where could it be?'

'Gee, now I'm going to be in big trouble.'

Aunt Betty had already had the watch repaired, and he hadn't had it very long.

'Come on, maybe she won't notice. We can check the clock in the living room. And besides that's the least of our worries.'

Tristan led the way out of the woods. They ran as fast as they could, the thick grass hindering their progress. Tristan had a feeling they would be grounded forever after staying out all night. Aunt Betty must be beside herself.

They found Aunt Betty stretched out in her favourite recliner. Feet up, a book open face down on her lap, and a snore here and there escaping.

She woke to Gertrude and Tristan arguing about the time.

'It can't be tomorrow; we left after one o'clock. Now it's only two o'clock. It takes a good half hour to get back from the Woods.'

'Of course, it can't be tomorrow because it is today,' Aunt Betty replied as she wiggled into a better sitting position.

Tristan and Gertrude spun around to face Aunt Betty. Both with hung heads waited for the onslaught that was to come.

But Aunt Betty said nothing except. 'You two are back early again. Don't you enjoy the outdoors?'

Tristan brow furrowed. He was rather confused.

'Yes,' he answered. He looked at Gertrude who wore a simple bemused expression.

Aunt Betty struggled out of her seat. 'How does a nice cup of tea and a slice of bread with my freshly made jam sound,' said Aunt Betty as she waddled into the kitchen.

'Yes please,' said Gertrude.

Tristan sat at the kitchen table rubbing his wrist. He didn't even realise he was doing it until Aunt Betty sat beside him.

'Where is your watch, dear?'

Tristan looked across at Gertrude for guidance. Looked back at Aunt Betty, then blurted out, 'it fell off my wrist. The band must be faulty.' He nodded his head at his own lie. Trying to convince himself as well as Aunt Betty. Aunt Betty sat silently for a while, which usually wasn't a good sign.

'My dear boy, I can't understand for the life of me how a brand-new watch could come undone all by itself. Here are the rules. Find the watch before the sun sets, and no harm done. If not I'm afraid a week away from any activity you enjoy will commence tonight.'

Tristan hung his head disappointed. He knew he wouldn't be able to find the watch. That watch caused him more harm than good, he thought. Though he had become better at showing up on time for Mr. James and his farm lessons. Something he enjoyed.

'Let's go, Tristan, we can both look for your watch,' said Gertrude, taking her cup and plate to the sink. Tristan was still moping; he didn't see the point. The watch wasn't going to suddenly appear, was it? It had just vanished into thin air. But he knew he had to at least pretend he was looking for it and then take his punishment. He was upset more because he hadn't done anything wrong this time and was still going to miss out on the things he enjoyed.

He rose from the table and mechanically followed Gertrude out the kitchen door. Gertrude was smiling as they walked back past Carmel's barn on the way to the woods.

'What are you smiling about,' Tristan spat, annoyed. How could you be so happy? Just because I'm grounded and you're not. It doesn't mean you have to be quite so happy.'

'Oh, sorry Tristan. I feel ever so bad about your watch missing, truly I do.'

'You told me to leave it there. It's your fault, but I'm getting punished.' Tristan stopped in his tracks. 'I'm not going all the way back to the woods when we both know it isn't there.'

'Just stop talking Tristan,' said Gertrude, grabbing Tristan on the shoulder, looking squarely in the eyes. 'I'm smiling because now we know we can stay much longer at Hollow Woods and not be missed.'

Tristan stared back at Gertrude, a smile forming on his face when he realised what Gertrude meant. But the smile was short-lived. 'But I'm grounded, and you're not.'

'Don't worry. I'll make a pledge to you,' she said, holding her hand across her heart. 'I will never visit Hollow Woods without you.'

'Really?'

'Really, we are grounded together.'

With that, Tristan lifted Gertrude in a bear hug, twirled her around and they both fell on the ground in a laughing heap.

Chapter 19

The last day of the week-long punishment had finally come, and Aunt Betty had continually made her point. Each time Tristan asked to do something, anything, like help make scones, or build his model plane, or fly his kite, she gave him the same response. No.

Tristan was starting to get bored. The only things he was allowed to do were clean up his room, tend to the vegetable patch near the kitchen door, prepare the fields with Mr. James' help, and attend their morning lessons. He was glad about one thing; it was his birthday tomorrow. The very first birthday held outside of the orphanage. Aunt Betty or Gertrude hadn't mentioned it, and he was wondering if they even knew he would be turning thirteen tomorrow.

He pondered the notion of what tomorrow would be like if he were still in the orphanage. He imagined that the cranky old matron would be pulling him out of bed by the ear, as she had often done. And continued to drag him all the way down the draught-ridden hallway to start his chores in the kitchen.

He had the chore of cooking breakfast for more than thirty boys and the ungrateful Matron Collins. Each morning, she would complain about his cooking. But what more could he do with the little food he was given? There was not much you could do with oats. He was glad he now lived on the farm he could sleep a bit longer. And that Aunt Betty fed them well.

***

Tristan woke with a start something was wetting his face. He thought it was part of his dream at first. Still, with his eyes closed, he was trying to push whatever was away.

'Surprise,' yelling Aunt Betty and Gertrude. They sat on either side of Tristan's bed making it hard for him to wriggle out of the sheets. His eyes only half-open. Tristan still wanted to sleep and then he remembered. It was his birthday, and his eyes widened, taking in what was happening around him.

'Look what I have for you, my dear boy, Aunt Betty said, handing him a honeycomb-coloured puppy. 'She's from the litter Molly had. It was her last litter, so Mr. James told me.'

'Happy birthday,' said Gertrude handing Tristan a handmade card. Gertrude had decorated the card. It had a drawing of a boy and a dog, with the farm in the background.

'Thank you, Aunt Betty, thank you, Gertrude, this is the first birthday card I have ever received.'

Aunt Betty and Gertrude looked at each other in disbelief.

'And the first, and best present I could ever have,' he said squeezing the dog close to him. Tristan was happier than he could ever be, but he said, 'I'm not even sure that today is my real birthday. Only from what the Matron at the orphanage told me,' his tone a bit demure.

'Well, my boy, it is. Among the official

documentation given to me from the orphanage, today is indeed your birthday.'

'Oh, wow. My real birthday,' he said, and they all started to laugh.

Aunt Betty made Tristan the biggest and best breakfast he had ever had. On two slices of toast sat creamy scrambled eggs, with a dollop of butter, and one rasher of bacon. Aunt Betty had also declared it a lesson-free day. Who wants to do lessons on their birthday, she had said?

After breakfast, Tristan, with Gertrude following, took his new puppy out into the yard to commence her training. Tristan stood on the grassy area between the back door and the clothesline.

'She needs a name before you can start training her.'

Gertrude was right he thought, but what? The puppy had been under their feet a moment ago. And when Tristan looked around, she was trying to tug one Aunt Betty lovely yellow daisies out of a pot near the back door.

'I know,' he said, rescuing the flowers pushing

them back into the soil. 'Her name is Daisy.'

'Perfect,' agreed Gertrude. Tristan picked up his new puppy and said, 'Hello Daisy,' and she licked him on the nose.

Tristan found some rope in the barn which he made into a collar and lead. Tristan took Daisy to the top of the long driveway and commenced walking Daisy up and down. On the fifth lap Gertrude gave up and went back into the house. But Tristan continued until he eventually took off the lead, and the puppy followed him back and forth all on her own.

***

'Do you think he will like it?' asked Gertrude as she helped Aunt Betty put the finishing touches on the birthday cake they had made for Tristan. He was still outside playing with his puppy, Daisy.

'I believe he will love it,' exclaimed Aunt Betty. She looked proudly at their creation taking centre place in the middle of the kitchen table. 'Call him in, will you dear.'

Gertrude opened the front door and yelled out to

Tristan to come in.

'I didn't mean for you to holla, dear girl.'

'Sorry,' Gertrude grimaced.

Tristan burst through the kitchen door with Daisy underfoot.

'She seems to have taken to you, my boy. She's following you around nicely. I believe if you're persistent with her training, she'll make a fine companion.'

Tristan hadn't seen the cake yet. Gertrude and Aunt Betty were standing in front of it.

'We have one more present for you,' said Aunt Betty. And they both moved away to reveal the cake.

Gertrude watched Tristan's reaction. It was exactly as she expected. A big grin formed on his face along with a tear of happiness slipping down his cheek.

'Wow, my very own birthday cake. And look how big it is.' Tristan moved closer and sniffed it. 'It smells delicious.'

'It's your favourite. Chocolate.' Gertrude said.

'Can we have some now?' he asked Aunt Betty

who was standing proudly next to Gertrude.

'Why not?' she said.

Gertrude and Aunt Betty sang their best rendition of the birthday song, While Tristan gulped in a huge amount of air and blew out all thirteen candles. He devoured two large servings of cake with an extra-large dollop of cream, then they sat in the living room, content and full. Daisy fell asleep on Tristan's lap.

Gertrude smiled. She felt happy for Tristan being able to celebrate his birthday like other children.

Chapter 20

Tristan had spent most of that week training Daisy at every opportunity he had. Gertrude had to find other things to do by herself because he was too busy with the puppy. She could see how determined he was to train Daisy to be obedient, but she felt a bit left out.

Gertrude was aching to get back to Hollow Woods and visit with her friends. She also wanted to have a better look around for Tristan's watch, surely it must be there somewhere? She had thought a lot about it and wondered if an animal in the Woods had grabbed it. How else would it just disappear?

She managed to drag Tristan into her room telling Aunt Betty she needed Tristan's help with a mathematics question she was trying to work out. Which was kind of true, as he was much better with numbers than her.

'Which question are you stuck on?' asked Tristan as he followed her to her room. Gertrude ushered him in and shut the door.

'I don't really need your help with mathematics. I think I know the answer.'

'What then?' said Tristan. Gertrude sat on the edge of the bed, and Tristan sat beside her.

'I want to go to Hollow Woods and see our friends. But this time I want to stay longer.'

'Oh, no, no, I can't leave Daisy. She needs me.' Gertrude rolled her eyes.

'She won't even know you're gone. Remember, the time doesn't change here when we enter Hollow Woods. Gertrude could see Tristan was thinking about it.

'But I will know,' he finally said. Gertrude shook her head frustrated, now Tristan has a puppy his interest in Daisy is more important than their friends and her.

'Aren't you eager to see Logan and practice archery?' Gertrude was hoping that would sway him.

'Yes,' he said. 'But what about Daisy?'

'That's it. I promised I wouldn't go to Hollow Woods without you while you were grounded. You're not grounded anymore. Tomorrow I'm going with or without you. I'm also planning to stay longer. So, if you're coming, you better pack a bag.'

'How long?'

Gertrude just shrugged her shoulder, opened the door, and went back out to the living room.

'Did you work out your mathematics question, dear?'

'Yes, Aunt Betty, I think I did.

***

The very next day after Gertrude milked Carmel and had her breakfast, she gathered some clothes ready for her next visit to Hollow Woods. She shoved them in a small backpack before hiding them under her bed. She was still angry with Tristan. Firstly, on account of her sacrificing time, she could have spent with her friends, Summer, Lily, and Jasmin, because he was grounded. And for him, spending far too much time with Daisy. She thought he was ever so selfish.

After their usual morning lessons with Aunt Betty and before lunch, Gertrude had the opportunity to fetch her backpack and sneak out the kitchen door. She held her bag in front of her. If Aunt Betty happened to look out of the window, she wouldn't be able to see it. She dumped it just around the corner of the barn so as she walked past on her way to Hollow Woods, she could grab it.

In the end, she had not packed much, simply because she didn't have many clothes. Aunt Betty had bought a few clothes for around the farm, including her overalls, which she loved the best, and a few dresses for church, but they weren't suitable for Hollow Woods.

Aunty Betty was in the kitchen vigorously stirring a cake mixture; she was making a cake for the next Oakdale County Show. Tristan sat at the table with Daisy leaning against his leg, her tail wagging. She was a delightful dog, thought Gertrude as she sat next to Tristan and petted Daisy.

'I'm going for a wander down by the brook after

lunch if it was alright with you Aunt Betty?' Gertrude wasn't just asking permission she was warning Tristan that he better makes up his mind soon or she would go without him.

'Yes, dear, it's a lovely day for a stroll. Are you going too?' she asked Tristan.

Tristan looked from Aunt Betty, Gertrude and then Daisy. Gertrude could plainly see he hadn't thought about it at all. He finally blurted out, 'I'm not sure, I'll think about it over lunch.' Aunt Betty stopped mid-stir and looked at Tristan, her head slightly tilted to one side as if observing him.

'Why don't you leave Daisy with me while you and Gertrude go and explore the brook? You haven't used your fishing rod for a while.'

'Perhaps,' was all he said before he picked his puppy up and gave her a hug.

Chapter 21

'Oh, I see you decided to come too, have you?' Gertrude looked down at Daisy. 'You should have tied her up. She can't come through the door. She might react differently to shrinking.'

'I'll send her home when Gilmyer opens the door,' he said, pulling the strap of his bag back over his shoulder.

'You're rather bossy today.' They made their way to the door in silence. Gertrude was still very cross with him. And now he had the dog in tow. What was he thinking?

Tristan knocked on the door, three sharp raps. 'Home Daisy, home,' he said, as Gilmyer opened the door. But Daisy darted through the door before Tristan had a chance to grab her. She yelped as she started to shrink and took off on the path towards the village.

'Sorry, Gilmyer. 'She's my new puppy,' Tristan quickly explained and started chasing her. Gertrude shook Gilmyer's hand.

'Animals aren't safe here. The Trolls will get her.'

'Oh dear,' she said and began chasing after Tristan and his dog.

'Hello, Logan,' Tristan called, not wanting to stop and explain what he was doing.

'Hey, what's the hurry?'

'My dog followed me in. I must find her,' he said, as Gertrude caught up with him.

'Hi Logan, we have to catch Daisy the Trolls might get her.'

'What?' said Tristan, his brow furrowed.

'The gate is locked. The Trolls can't get in unless they're invited. Come on, I have a surprise for you. We can find Daisy later.' Logan wasn't too concerned, so Gertrude thought Gilmyer was exaggerating.

'What is it, Tristan replied eagerly as he looked back towards the path Daisy had taken.

'This. It's a part of Hollow Woods that not many of the elves visit, but it is so fascinating. Follow me.' Logan led them up a narrow sloping track covered with weeping trees. Further along the track, two young male elves joined them from behind.

'Who are you?' Gertrude asked, turning to look behind her.

'The short stumpy one is Oscar, and the long, lanky one is Vinnie,' Logan answered for them.

'Why haven't we met you before,' asked Gertrude as her curiosity peeked.

'Um, a Bax, I mean…,' said Oscar.

'Oscar, means to say that he has been busy in the fields churning the soil for the next crop,' said Logan.

The path wound up and then down to a dilapidated wooden bridge. Across the bridge seemed to be nothing but darkest. A dark grey cloud hung above. There were no flowers or shrubs, and the trees that were there looked dead and limp. On this side of the bridge, everything seemed to flourish. That's peculiar, thought Gertrude.

'What is this place?' asked Gertrude.

'This is where we take nosy people and lock them away,' said Logan as he turned toward Gertrude and Tristan with an evil glare. Both Vinnie and Oscar formed a line standing either side of Logan, preventing Gertrude and Tristan from returning from where they came.

'Quit it will you, Logan, you're scaring me,' said Tristan grabbing hold of Gertrude's hand.

'This is the end of the road for you two. No one ever escapes the Darkness,' he said. He, Oscar, and Vinnie grabbed the pair and started pushing them across the bridge, towards the Darkness.

'I thought you were our friend,' Tristan said, as he twisted and turned, trying to get loose.

'Elves don't make friends, you silly boy,' Logan replied. They were halfway across the bridge when Gertrude heard a faint voice from the direction they had come.

'Look, it's Lily,' said Gertrude, pointing up the hill. Lily was waving her hands around, yelling something, but Gertrude couldn't quite make it out. Then Summer and Logan arrived beside Lily.

'But how could you be…,' said Tristan. 'Who are you?' Then Gertrude heard Logan's voice. 'Run, run that's Baxter. Run.'

Tristan kicked Oscar in the shin. He yelled out in pain and started hopping around holding his ankle. Gertrude elbowed Vinnie in the stomach, and he buckled over trying to get his breath back. They both ran as fast as they could toward the real Logan, Lily, and Summer.

'Are you alright?' said Summer, as Gertrude and Tristan reached them, both gulping in air to regain steady breathing.

'Gee, Logan, Baxter looks just like you,' Tristan said, staring at Logan and then back down the hill towards where Baxter and his goons were.

'Come on, you two, let's get you back to the Great Hall. We must inform Mortar,' Logan said leading the group back to safety. 'One minute Baxter is the hero, the next he's showing his nasty streak. This time he has gone too far. He has never been this horrible before though.'

They followed Logan down a different path to the

one Baxter had led them. Gertrude kept thinking how they wouldn't ever be able to tell Logan and Baxter apart. That could happen again, and something bad might happen to her and Tristan next time if their friends weren't around to save them. Aunt Betty would be devastated if they just disappeared, never to be found again. She was also wondering why Baxter was so mean. *Why was he like that?*

'My dog, Daisy. She followed me in.'

'We must find her the Trolls will eat her. But first I need to see Mortar.'

***

They found Mortar sitting on his Throne rocking and cooing at the newest elf baby of the Hollow Woods Community. Gertrude could see how much of a softy he was.

'Father, we have some dire news,' said Logan, as he bowed his head. Mortar handed the child back to its mother and asked the other subjects to clear the room.

'What could be so dire in Hollow Woods?' said Mortar, as he stood and stretched, taking in a deep breath.

Logan said one word. 'Baxter.'

'What is he up to now?'

Logan went on to describe what took place and the more he spoke, the bigger the frown on Mortar's face.

'Father, you know if he succeeded in getting Gertrude and Tristan across the bridge to the Darkness they would have been gone forever.'

'We would have?' asked Tristan, swallowing a lump of newfound fear as Logan nodded.

Gertrude was starting to think that Hollow Woods had a few secrets she was keen to unravel.

Mortar apologised to Gertrude and Tristan and assured them it wouldn't happen again. 'This time, he has gone too far,' said Mortar.

'But how will we know if it is Logan or Baxter?' asked Gertrude.

'There are two ways you can make sure you are talking to me. Firstly, see here,' Logan said, pointing to a two-inch scar on the left side of his chin which ran down the edge of his jaw line. Gertrude and

Tristan moved closer to look at it.

'And what's the other way,' said Tristan.

'What about if each time we meet we have a special handshake like this?' Logan grabbed Tristan's right hand, shook it three times, then spun around once and winked.

'Wow, that's great. But what if I forget it?'

'We will practice it soon,' said Logan.

'Mortar, your mightiness,' Tristan said and grimaced at what he was about to say. 'My dog Daisy followed me in, I need to find her.'

'That is a bit of a bother,' said Mortar. 'You must hurry and find her. We usually report breaches like this to the Council of The Four Lands.'

Chapter 22

The group of friends spent the afternoon helping Tristan search for Daisy. They looked everywhere. They checked the south gate to Mount Golmargret where the Dwarfs lived, and the western entrance to The Dolan Thickets where the Goblins lived.

'Look,' said Tristan, pointing to the barred gate that led east to The Tower of Zebajin where the Trolls lived. 'What if Daisy squeezed through here,' he said pointing to the bottom of the gate. Gertrude surveyed it and cringed. The thought of those ugly looking Trolls eating an innocent puppy made her want to vomit.

'There are plenty of places besides here where Daisy could have gone,' grimaced Logan, trying to reassure his friend. 'Come on, let's update Mortar. I'm sure Daisy will turn up when she is hungry.'

'Well, I hope the Trolls aren't hungry yet,' Tristan said, hanging his head as they made their way over to Mortar.

Mortar was sitting on the steps of the Great Hall talking to an owl. Both Tristan and Gertrude looked at each other in wonderment.

'Why are you talking to an owl?' Tristan blurted out.

'This is my adviser, Tutu.'

'Hello, Tristan and Gertrude,' said Tutu. 'Did you find your dog?'

'No, but... no way. You, it, how can it talk?' Tristan said. He looked at Mortar and then at the owl for an answer. Gertrude was just as entranced as Tristan.

'Tutu is the last of his kind in Hollow Woods and has been my companion and adviser for over one hundred years. We have been together since childhood.'

'But how can he talk?' asked Gertrude.

'All Ancient Owls talk, and they know more than

one language. Tutu here also speaks the lost tongue of our ancestors,' said Mortar. Summer and her friends left Tristan and Gertrude to chat with Mortar and Tutu.

'See you at Twilight,' said Logan, waving as he walked down the stairs hand in hand with Summer.

'We have been studying the Italian language at home,' Gertrude piped up. 'Listen. *Uno, due, tre, quattro, cinque, sei, sette, otto, nove diece.*'

'Bravo,' said Tutu and then he whispered in Mortar's ear.

'Excellent idea, Tutu. I have decided you can help Tutu transfer the Ancient Scrolls to the tongue we now speak. And in doing so, you will come to understand our people,' he said to Gertrude.

Gertrude smiled in acceptance. 'Thank you Mortar, it is a privilege.'

'Let's commence now,' said Tutu. Tutu took flight and Gertrude followed him towards the library, through a large archway on the other side of The Great Hall.

'What, aren't you going to help me find Daisy?'

Tristan yelling after her.

'We have looked everywhere,' she replied and continued with Tutu to the library.

'Well, I am,' said Tristan, and with that, he took off towards the kitchen to look for Daisy.

Gertrude sat at a large table where a long scroll made of parchment with words she didn't understand had been spread across the length of the table. Tutu perched on the back of the chair beside her. The first thing Tutu taught Gertrude was the Ancient Song.

'This song is so strong that in times of trouble it could save Hollow Woods.' Tutu read the words to Gertrude.

> *The Moon it rides above the wind,*
> *To ensure the earth is well aligned.*
> *The Tulips bring our season in,*
> *And welcome in our next of kin.*
> *The rising Sun warms our hearts,*
> *And guides us through the Ancient charts.*
> *Bring this combination to accord,*
> *Hollow Woods must be restored.*

'It's beautiful. But how can a song save Hollow Woods?'

'Oh, it's a beautiful story, said to be sung by the High Elf herself Gaylia over one thousand years ago when a civil war was at a point where extinction was a real possibility. Gaylia had so much love in her heart for the elves, so she sang it over and over until a great peace laid its hand on all The Four Lands. Never again have we witnessed such a war since.'

Gertrude thought about what Tutu had just shared with her and felt honoured that Tutu thought she would be a worthy candidate to learn such a special song.

'Wasn't there a war about three hundred years ago,' she asked.

'Yes, but it was short. Banishing the humans saw that war come to a halt immediately.'

'It seems like everything is very old here?' Gertrude said. She wrote the words of the song in English so she could practice it at home.

'Yes, we are. We all live a long life here. I believe another copy of this song is in *The Book of Dawning*.

The owl fluttered off, making his way to the second aisle. Three aisles sat in the middle of the library from roof to floor full of scrolls. After Gertrude finished rewriting the Ancient Song, she joined Tutu.

'What are you looking for?' she asked.

'Tutu was perched on the end of a heavy scroll scratching his brow with tip of his wing. 'I don't understand, *The Book of Dawning* should be right here.'

Gertrude looked around at the multitude of scrolls. 'How can you tell which one is which?' she asked.

Tutu didn't answer her immediately but jumped about from one bay to the next. 'Um, perhaps you should visit with Summer while I have a more thorough look,' was his reply.

Chapter 23

Tutu burst into the Throne Room where Mortar was having a well-earned nap. He was lounging on the gold-coloured double cushion settee when Tutu abruptly woke him.

'Master, master, you must come to the library immediately.'

'Why is everyone in a rush lately?' Mortar raised his hands above his head, stretching to full length as he stood and yawned. 'Tutu, you pick the worst time to interrupt me, I was about to win the archery contest. I have never won it in real life.'

Tutu clicked his tongue. 'This is far more important, dear sir, than any tournament. Come, I'll explain when we get to the library; these walls may have ears.'

Mortar pushed the double doors open and entered the library with Tutu flying by his side. Once they were both inside, he shut the doors gently and turned to Tutu.

'Now my dearest and oldest friend, what is so secret?'

'Enough of the old bit if you don't mind, Master. I have searched everywhere, and I can't find *The Book of Dawning*.'

'Are you sure?'

'Very sure. Though I have looked in other spots throughout the library, I always return it to aisle two, bay four, shelf five.'

Mortar followed Tutu as he fluttered about and landed on the shelf where the scroll should be. Mortar rummaged through each shelf reading each scroll's title. And indeed, it seemed that *The Book of Dawning* was missing.

'Who else knows?' Mortar asked, realising the impact it would have if the scroll landed in the wrong hands.

'Gertrude knows I was looking for it, but she doesn't know its significance.'

'Summons Logan and Summer. Get them to help with a search, and I want it done now.'

***

Summer was about to show Gertrude her scrying stones, which gave her the ability to observe The Four Lands when she puts her mind to it. One of Mortar's guards entered Summer's hut. He whispered someone into Summer's ear. She excused herself, suggesting Gertrude help Tristan find Daisy.

There seemed to be a lot of kerfuffle today, thought Gertrude. Firstly, they had an altercation with Baxter, Daisy ran off somewhere, and now Summer was summoned to see Mortar.

What's happening? She made her way to the courtyard as most of the Elves were doing. It was coming on Twilight.

'I see you found Daisy,' said Gertrude as she squeezed in next to Tristan and Lily.

'Do you know why Summer was asked to see Mortar?' Gertrude asked Lily.

'No, I don't. Logan was summoned too,' she replied.

Gertrude was about to ask another question, but the chanting began.

***

Mortar stood at the door of the library watching Tutu, Summer, and Logan scoured through the many shelves in the library picking each scroll up and reading the title out aloud before replacing it on the shelf.

'It's not here, Father,' said Logan. He had looked at the final scroll in the aisle he was checking. Mortar scratched his head. He was becoming more and more concerned about the incidents that have continued to occur now that Gertrude and Tristan were part of their community.

Have I made the right decision he thought? Another concern which troubled him deeply was Baxter. He understood his son's struggle with the death of his mother, the loss had always affected him deeply. But Mortar also knew it was coming to the point of announcing the date of the new leadership where he will take his leave and retire. He just can't see Baxter in that role, though he was the firstborn.

'Nothing, Master,' said Tutu, bringing Mortar back to the present. Mortar had no choice. 'Send word to Bostrabelle, Rakash, and Zrork, let them know a special meeting of The Four Lands will take place at high sun, two moons from now. Logan, arrange permanent patrols at each of the gates as soon as the feast for twilight is over. Now go and eat, and not a word.'

Mortar sat for a long moment; his brow furrowed in thought.

'What is on your mind, Master,' Tutu asked, flying back to his side.

'I'm not sure. But all of this feels like the work of Folmar.'

'That's impossible! He has no way of escaping the Eternal Prism.'

Mortar shook his head as he rose from his chair, 'Nothing is impossible.'

'I hope you're wrong Master.'

Chapter 24

Tristan had just swallowed his last mouthful of food when Logan tapped him on the shoulder.

'I see you found your dog.' Daisy had a rope secured around her neck, and the other end was held tightly by Tristan.

'Yes, she won't go anywhere without me.' Tristan stood and rubbed his belly. His once scrawny build was starting to fill out. He had never imagined life outside of the orphanage. But here he was in Hollow Woods, feasting until he was full.

'I need your help, Tristan. I'm on patrol tonight checking the west and east sides of Hollow Woods; care to join me?'

Tristan's chest puffed out. 'Be honoured. Can I bring Daisy?'

'Of course. Come on, this way.'

Tristan followed Logan past the bridge where Baxter and his goons had tricked him and Gertrude only that morning.

'Hey, prove you are Logan,' Tristan said, stopping abruptly. Logan stepped towards Tristan. He grabbed Tristan's right hand, shook it three times, spun around once, and winked.

Tristan still wasn't convinced. The bridge to the Darkness was a stone's throw away.

'Show me your scar.' Logan jutted out his chin and held the burning torch he was carrying closer. 'Yep, that's you. I'm right to go now,' he said, satisfied it was Logan. They followed a narrow path, with some parts of it so narrow they had to turn sideways.

'Remind me to call the maintenance crew here to cut back a few of these trees?' Logan was a lot bigger than Tristan and the branches scratched at his bare arm as he squeezed through.

There were no real boundary fences that Tristan could see. The east side boundary was lined with a double row of towering trees.

'How are those trees going to stop anyone from

entering Hollow Woods?' asked Tristan.

Logan considered his response for a moment. 'To you, they look like a few rows of trees.' Logan moved closer to the trees. 'Try and walk past the trees. Slowly though,' Logan warned, taking hold of Daisy.

Tristan brow furrowed. *Was something going to happen to him?* He trusted his friend, Logan. He walked towards a small gap between and trees, kicked his toe on something hard. Then, knocked his head.

'What was that?' he said, rubbing his forehead.

'Sorry, Tristan. It was easier to show you.'

'Easier for you, he said, taking Daisy back.'

'This invisible boundary is connected to the main dome that protects Hollow Woods. It can be breached with certain ancient spells. But it is unlikely.'

'Spells! Do you know any spells?'

'Only what I need to know. Come on. We still have the west side and Armory to check.

The west side boundary looked like the east side, though the trees were thicker in places. Several large statues of Elves made with a concrete-looking substance stood in front of a line of trees. They were all peering at Tristan. It gave him the creeps.

'Who are they?' Tristan said, pointing.

'These statues represent previous leaders. All brave warriors. Our history hasn't always been peaceful.'

'So, will there be a statue of Mortar one day?'

'Yes. It's custom for the statue to be made at the beginning of leadership. Father's is safely stored in the Throne Room.'

'Who was the leader before Mortar?'

'My father was voted in by the elf clan and the council of The Four Lands after Folmar, the High Wizard, went rogue.'

'A Wizard? Which one is he?' Tristan said, nodding towards the statues. 'And what did he do?'

Logan suddenly looked sad. Tristan waited for his friend to respond. Logan sat on a weather-worn fallen tree trunk, and Tristan sat beside him.

'Folmar became greedy and selfish in his position as leader. He caused the last war which saw the humans banished. He was the reason my mother lays in death.'

'Sorry, Logan, I didn't mean to upset you.' Tristan

felt awful, bringing up bad memories for his friend.

'Baxter has always blamed the humans. But the humans were Folmar's pawns, under his spell. You can see why Baxter acted in the way he did today, but that was too much. He has never been that bad or horrid.'

They continued towards the west side Armory, the last place to check. It was a large building spanning the size of a soccer field. Logan lit the torches along the right-side wall as they walked deeper into the building. Rows and rows of arrows lay on benches. Bows hung on hooks on the walls ten deep. On the left were spears and arrows. And down the middle were workbenches.

Tristan had been wondering about Folmar. And finally asked, 'Where is Folmar now?'

Logan lit the final torch and responded. 'He is in exile. In the Eternal Prism. Floating and leading a life of nothingness.'

'Wow. That sounds awful. Folmar can't escape, can he?'

'He's getting less than he deserves, and will remain

there until the sun no longer rises, until the end of time.'

'Well, I know never to cross your lot,' Tristan said half-joking.

They waded through the many rows of half-made weaponry, and in the far corner, Tristan noticed the remnant of a fire. It must have been the fire Baxter spoke about and had put out. The charred remains spread over a few square feet with the primary source seemed to have started on a workbench. Logan picked up a spearhead using it to sift through the blackened objects.

A flicker of light from the torch landed on an item. Tristan reached in front of Logan to retrieve it.

'Wait a minute. Look,' Tristan said, holding the mangled metal up closer to the light. 'It's my watch. How on earth did it get here? I left it just outside the door in the woods. How bizarre!'

Tristan noticed that Logan hadn't said a word. That was usually a sign that Logan was thinking, a trait Tristan would like to acquire in time. He just blurted things out before thinking, which didn't always go down well. 'What's got your goat?' he asked Logan. He could see by Logan's vague expression that he didn't have a clue what he was talking about, so he rephrased it. 'What's on your mind?'

'Baxter.'

'Baxter?'

'Yes, it's all starting to make sense. Baxter must be behind all of this. Like I said, Baxter wouldn't normally try to scare someone like he did with you and Gertrude.'

'I wasn't that scared.' Logan gave him a look and shook his head. 'Perhaps a tiny little bit scared,' Tristan grimaced.

'I think Baxter took your watch and lied about seeing the Trolls. He lit this fire to cover his tracks. But what is he up too? Let's get back to the Throne room and report our findings to Mortar.

Chapter 25

Mortar paced the length of the Throne Room. The decision he was contemplating would drive a bigger wedge between his sons. But he knew his ruling had to be based on what was best for The Four Lands, not his family. The announcement of Baxter as the new leader was supposed to take place on the coming of the fourth full moon. But after hearing Logan's theory that Baxter was behind the upheaval, Mortar felt he had no choice.

Tutu interrupted his thoughts. 'Master from what Logan said and from what we have talked at length about tonight, we must address this at special meeting of The Four Lands.

'You're right, my wise friend.'

Mortar retired to his room. He lay watching the clouds in the darkened sky drift out of view. The lights flickered from the township below. It took a long time for him to find sleep. He woke several times, wishing his late wife was with him to help his family through yet another divide.

Mortar wished to wake early and talk with Baxter and gauge his reaction to the announcement he would soon deliver. He wanted this announcement to be light-hearted as though it was Baxter's wishes and Baxter's choice. That way, thought Mortar, it would save Baxter from any embarrassment.

As the sun crept into his room Mortar stretched his tall form and sat on the side of the bed. He made his way to the Throne Room where Tutu was studying one of the scrolls from the library.

'Good Dawning to you, Master.'

'And to you,' Mortar replied. 'What are you looking at, dear friend?'

'Well, in light of your announcement, I thought it would be a good idea to check the rules regarding denouncing the next leader.'

Mortar looked over Tutu feathered shoulder and read the section Tutu had indicated. After reading it, Mortar scratched his head and said, 'surely, I don't have to stick to that. It will shame my son.'

'I'm afraid you do. If you don't, anyone of the other lands will be voted in.'

'We must find Baxter. Send Gilmyer out to find him. And have Logan summoned, to see me.'

***

Mortar sat nervously as the leaders from the other lands entered The Great Hall. Rakash from the east and The Tower of Zebajin, the leader of the Trolls sat at the meeting table diagonally opposite Mortar. Bostrabelle from the south and Mount Golmargret, the leader of the dwarfs took the vacant seat next to Mortar and nodded to him. And lastly, Zrork from the west and of the Dolan Thicket, the leader of the Goblins sat beside Rakash.

Being a special meeting, only those involved were present. Mortar had spoken to Logan and told him of his decision and Logan had reluctantly agreed to stand as leader of the Elves.

But Mortar had had no time to warn Baxter of his announcement. Baxter arrived just before the meeting when the main doors were about to close. Mortar signalled with his hand to Baxter to come to him. He needed to talk to his son. He needed to warn him of how upsetting it would be for him. But he could see Baxter's stance indicated his bad mood.

The four leaders sat facing each other. Fruit platters lay along the centre of the table. Logan stood beside his father and Tutu, who was perched on the back of Mortar's chair. Baxter stood close to the door looking like that was the last place he wanted to be.

The leader of the Trolls commanded silence in the room. 'I'm surprised the humans, and their mangy dog aren't in the room. They are the cause of the recent trouble,' said Rakash.

Zrork, the leader of the Goblins, sniggered at the remark.

Mortar shook his head. 'No, Rakash, the humans aren't a bother at all. And we found the dog before you lot gobbled her up.'

'How dare you,' rumbled Rakash, slamming his fist

on the table.

Bostrabelle sat opposite Rakash and stood on her chair. 'That's enough, both of you. Let's stick to what is important. Mortar, why have you called this Special Meeting?'

Mortar took in a deep breath. He was feeling like a failure to his people and his sons lately and having to make these announcements now shamed him. 'As you all know, we pride ourselves on protecting the people of The Four Lands and an incident has come to our attention.'

'Get to the point,' spat Zrork, the leader of the Goblins.

'Over the last few moons or so a few odd things have been happening. One twilight, we believe our boundaries were breached,' Mortar said looking directly at Rakash. 'Tristan's new watch went missing. He had left it outside in the woods. A fire was reported on the same twilight as the boundary breach in the west side Armory. And that is where Tristan and Logan found the watch while on patrol.'

'Why was a human on patrol?' demanded Zrork.

Logan spoke up now, 'Tristan has become a true friend and has learned archery in the short time he has been welcome to Hollow Woods.'

'How nice. A true friend,' grumbled Rakash.

'I would trust him with my life,' retorted Logan.

Bostrabelle broke through the heated discussion that followed with her warning horn. 'These incidents hardly give reason for a Special Meeting of the council, Mortar,' Bostrabelle said once the room was hushed.

'Yes, well, there is one more, the dog Daisy was lost for a while as you know.' Mortar straightened his posture and announced. 'But one of the reasons you have been called to this meeting to is that *The Book of Dawning* is missing.'

There, I've said it, he thought.

'Are you sure,' asked Bostrabelle.

'What kind of leader are you?' said Rakash.

Mortar knew he would get this reaction, particularly from Rakash. He had always argued that the Trolls should lead The Four Lands. But all the other races knew that if that ever happened, their existence would be pilfered. And that was why Mortar was at odds with his decision about Baxter.

'Yes, I'm sure,' Mortar replied to Bostrabelle, ignoring Rakash.

'What action should we put in place to find *The Book of Dawning*?' asked Zrork.

'I request that each leader arrange a thorough search of all its people's belonging.'

'Surely it must be here in Hollow Woods,' questioned Rakash.

'Perhaps it is,' Mortar replied. 'There is one more matter I wish to present to the council.' Mortar shifted uneasily in his seat. And he paused for a moment to gather the best words for what was about to be said. He looked at Logan for reassurance and then to Baxter, who still looked bored with the whole meeting.

'Firstly, in four moons, I will be retiring as leader of the Elves and The Four Lands.' He grimaced as he watched Baxter. His stance had changed to tall and proud, expectant of his birthright. 'And after careful thought and deliberation with my trusted adviser I announce Logan, the next leader.'

Mortar waited for the news to sink in. The room buzzed with discussion until Baxter yelled at the top of his voice.

'I'm the rightful Ruler, not Logan.'

Everyone looked across at Baxter as he approached the four seated council members and gave Logan a look of hatred. 'It is by law that I gain the position of leader, not the second-born,' he spat.

Mortar again searched for the right words. And he spoke gently to his son. 'I had Gilmyer search for you this dawning so I could talk with you before my announcement. You are distant from your people, and your heart has hardened.'

Baxter's face was reddening, his nostrils flaring like a bull about to attack. But he stood and listened.

'There is a clause in the law which allows the leader to denounce the rightful heir on the grounds of incapacity to rule in a fair manner. Your attitude along with your recent trickery that could have harmed Gertrude and Tristan has led to this decision. I'm sorry, son.'

'No, no, no.' Baxter ranted. His fists immediately curled, his arms bent, ready to fight. 'Let's see who the best leader is,' he said through gritted teeth. He moved swiftly towards Logan and whacked him in the jaw, sending Logan backward. He wasn't quick enough to block the next blow and landed on the floor. Baxter kicked him in the ribs and was about to kick Logan again when two guards pulled him back.

'You will all pay for this,' he retorted as the guards dragged him out of the room.'

Chapter 26

Tristan stood in the cobblestone courtyard with Daisy beside him, waiting for Logan to exit the meeting. Two guards dragged Baxter out of the Great Hall. Baxter struggled loose and ran in the direction of the library. Tristan had left Gertrude in the library earlier studying one of the ancient scrolls.

Logan had told Tristan what would be announced at the special meeting and understood the reaction Baxter just displayed. But he was also proud and happy for his new friend.

The large wooden doors opened to the Great Hall. The leaders piled out, seeming in good spirits. Tristan picked up Daisy and held her close to him when the leader of the Trolls, Rakash, looked his way. Tristan was sure Rakash gave him a sinister smile.

Logan was last to exit and took the steps two at a time towards Tristan.

Just as Logan reached the last step, a loud noise filled the air. All the folks of Hollow Woods stopped what they were doing and looked to where the sound was coming from. Then Gilmyer came around the corner, shouting, 'Fire, fire in the library.'

'Gertrude,' shouted Tristan. Dropping Daisy to the ground, he started running to the library. But Logan and Gilmyer caught up with him before he had a chance to enter the building.

A crowd had gathered, including the four leaders, all standing as close as they dared to the burning building. Tutu fluttered back and forth, pacing. The fire spat flames from the back of the building, sending plumes of dark grey smoke in the sky like thunder clouds.

'I can't lose Gertrude; she's the only real sister I've had.' Tears ran freely down Tristan's cheeks.

It wasn't long before a large group of male elves had dragged a large water-filled hose up to the library and aimed a fountain of water towards the back of the building. There was only one way in and out of the building, the front entrance. Tristan watched it eagerly for any sign of Gertrude emerging.

'She might be hurt or have been overcome by smoke. I have to go in and get her,' Tristan sobbed.

'You'll do no such thing,' Mortar said, hugging the boy to him and handing him his dog. 'Gertrude is a sensible girl; she should be out any minute.'

That wasn't very reassuring for Tristan. He squeezed Daisy closer to him and petted her.

'Look,' someone in the crowd shouted. Tristan shoved Daisy into Logan's arms and pushed further to the front of the swollen crowd. A blackened figure appeared at the entrance of the library, crouching, and carrying a large load of scrolls.

'It's Gertrude,' shouted Tristan, and ran to help her. She staggered and fell to the ground before he reached her. A pile of scrolls lay beside her.

Tristan dropped to the ground pulling Gertrude close to him. He gently rocked her like a mother would a child. 'Gertrude, Gertrude, wake up. You must wake up,' he said as tears streamed down his face. But her eyes remained shut.

Summer had joined the rest of the crowd after coming from way down in the tulip fields. She hadn't heard the explosion or noticed the clouds of smoke.

'Stand back,' Summer commanded. She kneeled next to Tristan.

'Make her wake up,' Tristan begged, looking into Summer's eyes.

Summer grimaced. 'Let me just check. Summer held her index and middle fingers to Gertrude's neck to find a pulse. Then, she held her ear above Gertrude's mouth. 'She's breathing.'

Tristan let out a sigh of relief.

Mortar stood over them now. 'I'll take her to the infirmary.' He lifted her with ease and made his way back through the crowd with Summer, Tristan, and Logan following.

The elves, though quite primitive in the way they lived, had a unique way of healing. Evelyn, the Healer, cared for Gertrude throughout the next days and nights with Tristan, only leaving her side when necessary. Gertrude was placed in a transparent bubble that was pumped with oxygen, hoping to clear her smoke-filled lungs. On the fourth twilight she woke.

Gertrude propped herself up with a mountain of pillows behind her. She was feeling dizzy and lightheaded. But Evelyn had told her it would pass once she started to move around. She had just finished her first meal since she had woken when Mortar and Tutu burst through the infirmary door.

'I'm so relieved you are well now, young lady. You gave us all a terrible fright. Tristan was beside himself with panic,' said Mortar.

'Sorry,' she said, hanging her head like a scolded dog.

'Don't be sorry,' said Tutu, 'you were so brave and clever to remove the restricted scroll from the library.'

'Thank you,' said Mortar. 'Both you and Tristan have proved to be caring and trusted friends.'

Gertrude grinned at the praise she got from Mortar and Tutu.

'Did you see anyone else in the library,' asked Tutu. Gertrude thought back. She remembered that she was reading the scroll about the shield that protects Hollow Woods and how over the centuries it had been compromised. She had been alone in the library, which was often the case except when Tutu would give her a formal lesson. The explosion had come from the rear of the building, and someone would have had to pass her to get there. But she had been so engrossed in the scroll she had been studying that she hadn't noticed.

'No, I don't recall, sorry. Tutu, you know what I'm like when I'm studying.'

'Yes, you are rather intense.'

'Never mind,' said Mortar. 'We have a feast planned in your honour when you're in better wellness.'

Chapter 27

Gertrude was confined to the infirmary for another week. During that time, Tristan had been sworn in as Logan's second-in-command. Tristan was so excited he had hugged Logan in front of the whole elf community. He knew he had a home with Aunt Betty, but this was where he belonged. His pride showed in his stance and newfound confidence.

Tristan and Logan were to train and direct chosen candidates to become part of a new security squad. It had been many thousands of moons, so Mortar had told Tristan since an army had to be prepared. Mortar also mentioned that he still wasn't sure what or who the enemy is exactly.

It was mid-morning when they had assembled in the courtyard in front of The Great Hall. More than fifty elves stood in rows as Mortar descended the steps to greet them. Standing in the front line were Summer and Jasmin, as well as a few other girls of the clan. Tristan smiled to himself as Mortar walked through each line and thanked his citizens for helping to protect the people of Hollow Woods.

The training schedule that Logan had put together was intense and challenging, but Tristan could see the merit in it. Each morning on dawning, they would run five leagues, which Tristan thought was close to ten times a football field. After that they would practice archery and hand-to-hand combat.

Tristan led the archery group and found it rewarding to help others develop their skills. He was an excellent shot by now and very rarely missed his target.

'Rightio, you fellows, straighten your stance. Relax your shoulder, aim, fire.' Tristan stood to the left of his trainees when he saw Gertrude heading towards him. 'Carry on,' he said as he met Gertrude halfway. 'I see they have finally let you out of the infirmary.'

'I was starting to go crazy staring at the same wall.

Though, Evelyn insists that I take things slow for the next week or so. Oh, congratulations on your new role as second-in-command.'

'I feel like I have a purpose. And I'm pretty good at archery now.' Tristan couldn't believe the different turn his life had taken. If Aunt Betty had never requested two children to help her run the farm, he just shivered at the thought of what he would be doing this very minute. Probably scrubbing the floor in the bathroom.

'Have you and Logan found Baxter yet?'

'No, we haven't. I think it was Baxter who lit the fire.'

'Surely not.'

'He was fuming when they dragged him out of the meeting, and he did run in the direction of the library.'

'Well, I hope not; Mortar would be horrified and so worried for Baxter if that was true.'

Two moons later, Gertrude and Tristan entered the Great Hall for the feast in honour of Gertrude. The hall was already full of all their friends and the rest of the elf community. At the main table, Mortar and the leaders of The Four Lands stood and started to clap as Gertrude and Tristan took their place next to Summer and Logan.

Before the food was served, Mortar stood and held his hand in the air waiting for the crowd to quieten. 'Dear friends, family, and guests, I'm so very proud of Gertrude and how brave she was to save some of our most important scrolls. Gertrude, please come here.'

Gertrude stood. She felt shy as she walked toward the main table with everyone paying attention to her, a twelve-year-old girl. She stood beside Mortar, who towered over her. When she had first met him, she was frightened of him, but not now, now that she knew him, not at all.

Mortar put his lanky arm around Gertrude's shoulder. 'This feast is to thank and honour Gertrude, our friend, for her bravery. Gertrude's brave act showed us how much she has come to care for us here in Hollow Woods. And because of her true loyalty I am honoured to award her with the Emblem of Peace.'

All who were present stood and clapped and started a chant, Gertrude had never heard before.

'Thank you, Mortar.'

Mortar placed the emblem around Gertrude's neck.

'The Emblem of Peace, as most of you know, belonged to Gaylia, the High Elf. Her love for her people, saved Hollow Woods. I believe Gertrude also has that love.' Everyone applauded again as Gertrude returned to her seat. After a while, the noise in the room fell to the hum of talk and laughter.

Gertrude looked down at the Emblem with humility and trepidation. Surely Mortar doesn't mean for her to be the one to save Hollow Woods one day? The feast was abundant with fresh vegetables and fruits served on large platters that sat in the middle of each table.

'Look at him,' said Tristan pointing to Rakash. 'He's not enjoying going meat-free, is he?' They all laughed at Tristan's comment and continued to eat.

Gertrude was starting to feel tired. She was still recovering, and the gathering had thinned. 'I need some rest,' she said, standing and yawning at the same time.

'Before you go,' said Summer, I have something for you.' Summer dragged three ruby-red stones from her pocket and handed them to Gertrude. Gertrude examined them moving them around in her hand. Though they were a deep red, they were clear like crystal but had smooth rounded edges.

'Thank you, but what are they?'

'They are scrying stones.'

Gertrude looked from Summer back at the stone. 'But what are they for?'

'I'll show you tomorrow, whatever you do don't lose one of them ever, or they won't work,' said Summer.

Gertrude looked down at the stones again. *Curious.* It looked like she would have to wait until tomorrow. She stowed the stones deep into the pocket of her tunic.

Chapter 28

Gertrude yawned and stretched as she woke from her slumber. Through her window, the sun indicated it was mid-morning. She had worn The Emblem of Peace to bed. And had sworn to herself she would never take it off, never. The emblem was mainly silver with an outline as black as the night. It had a hole in the middle surrounded by what looked like swirling vines.

When she arrived at her room last night, Gertrude had placed the three scrying stones on the table beside her bed. She had learned so much since she had arrived at the Appleton Farm and discovered Hollow Woods. Every morning on waking she would practice the song the High Elf, Gaylia, had used to save Hollow Woods.

The Moon it rides above the wind,
To ensure the earth is well aligned.
The Tulips bring our season in,
And welcome in our next of kin.
The Sun warms our hearts,
And guides us through the Ancient charts.
Bring this combination to accord,
Hollow Woods to be restored.

And now she was wearing The Emblem of Peace. She hoped she never had to use it! She dressed, ate some fruit for breakfast, pocketed the scrying stones and followed the path towards Summer's hut.

Summer was busy sweeping the floor when she arrived. 'Good dawning to you, Gertrude. Are you ready for your first scrying lesson?'

'To tell you the truth, I don't know.' Gertrude had no idea what she was about to learn, or what the stones were used for.

'Come on.' Summer led Gertrude to the living area of her hut and sat on the mat. It was one of the mats

Gertrude had worked on when she first came to Hollow Woods, which seemed such a long time ago. She sat opposite Summer. Summer offered her a cushion to sit on and put behind her back. She wriggled to get comfortable.

'The moons are aligning to show that you and Tristan will be a leading force in the future for Hollow Woods.'

'What? What does that even mean?'

'Well, since you and Tristan have connected with the elf community and Shandalar, Tutu has been reading the moon's shadow. The shadow gives an insight, though small, into what may happen in the future. Both you and Tristan are strong in our unfolding story of life.

'That is amazing. But you do know we are only kids.'

'The shadows tell only the truth.'

Gertrude was wondering about Baxter and whether the moon's shadows had revealed anything about him.

'Then why have all these things happened? Like

Tristan's watch disappeared and turned up mysteriously in the west side Armory, *The Book of Dawning* stolen. Baxter almost sending us to The Darkness, the security breach, and the fire in the library.'

'You do have a point. But the moon's shadow only reveals who will protect us, not what will happen. That is where the scrying stones come in. And why I have been asked by Mortar and Logan to teach you the art of scrying. Scrying helps you see what is happening to those you have a close connection with, and it does take some energy to execute a vision. We know it works for humans with a strong connection, and some elves have the ability can scry anyone in The Four Lands.

'So, can I spy on people? Like a crystal ball?'

'Yes, you can spy on people you have a connection with. But what is a crystal ball?'

'Never mind. Let's get started.' Summer explained to Gertrude the things she had to do to be able to scry.

'Firstly, lay the stone in front of you and begin by

just looking at the stones.'

'Yep, now what?'

'Now, think of someone you are close to and keep that thought purely on them.'

Gertrude thought of her mother first but abandoned that thought. She didn't want to find out this way whether her mother and father were still alive. Were they alive? She then shifted her thoughts to Aunt Betty. Last time she saw her, she was opening the door to the oven and was about to bring out a rich chocolate cake.

'Okay, I'm thinking of Aunt Betty. It doesn't have to be in Hollow Woods, does it?'

'No, it doesn't. Next, I want you to concentrate deeper.'

Gertrude wasn't at all sure of how to concentrate deeper, but she held her breath and stared hard at the stones, willing them to reveal a vision.

'Stop,' said Summer. 'You're going as red as your stones.'

'How else am I supposed to concentrate?' said Gertrude gulping some air.

'The art of scrying is close to when you fall into a dream state, so to do that, you must be relaxed as well. Watch me.' Summer placed her own stones in front of her. Then she closed her eyes and captured a thought of Logan. Next, she opened her eyes and focused on the stones. After a while she said, 'Logan should be knocking on my door now.'

Gertrude heard a tap on the door.

'Come in, Logan.'

'Have you been scrying me again?'

'Only to show Gertrude how it works,' she said, looking up and him.

'Wow, it really works.' Gertrude couldn't wait to learn to spy on everyone she had a connection with; this was going to be fun. Logan didn't stay long on account of Summer, telling him she was busy.

'Try again, but this time relax. Now I must tell you; you will know when a scry has broken through time when flecks of light appear in your stones.'

Gertrude tried to replicate what Summer had shown her earlier. She took a deep breath in and out. Closed her eyes and focused on Aunt Betty. Once she felt Aunt Betty was her only thought she opened her eyes and looked deep into the stones.

The stones started to show small flecks of light, which increased until they were a swirl of combined light and then it happened; she could see Aunt Betty.

Aunt Betty was standing by the kitchen sink, crying, her hand held under the tap with cold water running on it. She must have burnt herself, thought Gertrude. As soon as Gertrude's thought had shifted, she was pulled away from the vision. And she felt like she was falling backward.

As Gertrude came out of the scry, Summer was sitting behind her and caught her.

'Wow, that was amazing. I felt like I was falling back.'

'Yes, you do for the first few times, that's why I sat behind you. I ended up with a concussion from my first scry.'

'Thanks for saving me from that.'

'What did you see?'

'Aunt Betty, she has hurt herself. And I have just realised something.'

What is that?'

'That, even though time stands still out there in the real world, once we enter through the Door to Hollows, there is still a good half an hour from the time we leave the farm to get to the door. Anything could happen in that time.'

'Tristan and I must go back to the farm.'

Chapter 29

Gertrude and Tristan raced to the farm and found Aunt Betty in precisely the spot Gertrude had described in her visions.

'Wow, that's freaky stuff,' said Tristan as they piled through the door, with Daisy following. Aunt Betty tried to smile at them as they entered the kitchen, but it was more a grimace than a smile.

'Aunt Betty, are you all, right?' Gertrude said, realising it was a silly question.

'Well, my dear, I have been better,' she said through gritted teeth. 'I thought you had your horrid overall on when you left a while ago.'

'I'll fetch some ice,' suggested Tristan, not wanting Aunt Betty to notice his clothes, which were more like a Robin Hood outfit than farmwear. He raced to his room to get changed.

'You must have been mistaken,' said Gertrude, biting her bottom lip at the lie she had to tell. They had completely forgotten about changing when they knew Aunt Betty was hurt. And made a dash back to the farm without thinking. Gertrude made a mental note to remember their clothes for next time.

Gertrude helped Aunt Betty to her favourite chair in the living room after patting most of her hand dry. Her right hand was burnt from the index finger all along the edge to the tip of her thumb.

'How did you do this,' asked Gertrude. Tristan came in from the kitchen with a rather large piece of ice, as big as a golf ball. Gertrude gave him her look.

'What?'

'It's a bit big.'

'It'll last longer, won't it?'

'Good thinking, my boy,' said Aunt Betty, putting a told-you-so smile on Tristan's face.

'See,' he retaliated back at Gertrude. She rolled her eyes and got on with the job of making Aunt Betty comfortable. Gertrude and Tristan had decided to stay with Aunt Betty for a week before heading back to Hollow Woods.

Tristan wanted to get some wood chopped and check on the fences and see what else needed seeing to on the farm.

For the next week, they both worked together to get all the things done that Aunt Betty usually did in the house. Gertrude had concluded she and Tristan had taken things for granted on the farm and would make sure it wouldn't happen again.

Gertrude washed, folded, and ironed the clothes under the sometimes-annoying instruction of Aunt Betty. She milked Carmel, gathered eggs, watered the garden and pots surrounding the house, and cooked most of the meals.

Tristan, with Daisy at his heels, checked the fences, ploughed two fields, and started to fill the potted driveway with dirt. The wood he had cut was enough to last through to the next winter and then some, Aunt Betty, had said.

Each night while they were back on the farm, Gertrude would practice scrying. She had to wait until she could hear Aunt Betty snoring before she got the stones from inside one of her socks. She had shoved them to the back of her bottom drawer behind a wooden box she kept her treasures in, photos of her mother and father.

She had been trying to spy on Summer but couldn't seem to get one little spark of light from the stones. Perhaps, she was doing it wrong?

It was Friday afternoon when Aunt Betty waddled back up the driveway after collecting the mail. She had said she needed a walk and some fresh air. The ugly welts on her hand had started to heal.

As Aunt Betty walked through the door, she started opening the mail and reading it. She had carried the mail nestled in the apron she always wore. And would drag the letters out one-by-one to read them. Gertrude was sitting in the living room, trying her hand at knitting, which wasn't going very well. The lime green scarf she was working on was dotted with holes.

'How's your scarf coming along, dear?' Gertrude held the scarf up for Aunt Betty to inspect.

'Dear me. We might have to have another lesson soon.' Aunt Betty said as she continued to sift through the mail. Gertrude noticed her read the front and the back of one envelope and shoved it back into her pocket.

Hmm, I wonder who that letter was from?

Chapter 30

That night, when Aunt Betty had been snoring for some time, Gertrude sat cross-legged on the mat in the middle of her bedroom. The ruby stones sat in front of her. She had gone over and over in her head what Summer had taught her so far. *Maybe I'm not relaxed enough?*

She rolled her shoulder a few times and relaxed them. Then she took some deep breaths in through her nose and out through her mouth. Closing her eyes, she tried to clear her mind and think only of Summer. She remembered them together when Summer first showed her how to weave. She felt she had the connection now. She opened her eyes and looked deep into the scrying stones.

The stones started to flicker with light and then

swirls danced around inside them. She could see glimpses of Summer, but she wasn't sure where she was. It wasn't anywhere Gertrude had been in Hollow Woods. It looked like a cave, and it was well after twilight. The vision wasn't strong. But just as it faded, Summer was being dragged by a person Gertrude didn't recognise. *Oh, Summer's hands are bound.*

After coming out of the scry, Gertrude, worried and drained of energy snuck into Tristan's room.

Tristan wasn't the easiest person to wake. Gertrude tapped his arm gently but not a movement. So, she grabbed the pillow from under his head.

He sat upright, shaking himself awake. What? What's going on?' he said rather loudly. 'What are you doing in my room?' he demanded when he could see that Gertrude was sitting on his bed.

'Shhh, you'll wake Aunt Betty.

'Well, you woke me.'

'Shhh, keep your voice down. It's Summer. I think she is in danger.'

Tristan turned on the small lamp that sat on the table beside his bed and leaned against the bedhead.

'Are you sure?' Gertrude went through every detail with Tristan of what she had seen through the scrying stones.'

'Are you sure you didn't dream it or image it,' he said after she had finished.

'No. It was definitely a scry.'

'Well, I've patrolled most of Hollow Woods and haven't seen any place like that.'

'We need to get back to Hollow Woods tomorrow.'

Gertrude was up early as usual to milk Carmel. She was feeling extremely tired having not slept much. She was concerned for her friend and had realised the problems in Hollow Woods seem to be escalating.

Gertrude and Tristan had planned to leave straight after breakfast, telling Aunt Betty, they would check the fencing to the east of the property. It wasn't a total fib, and they knew that by the time they reached the entrance to Hollow Woods Mr. James, their neighbour, would be paying Aunt Betty a visit.

Aunt Betty had prepared breakfast now that her

hand was on the mend. They sat at the kitchen table, eating freshly baked bread topped thick with butter and homemade mulberry jam. Aunt Betty was looking a bit sheepish and was constantly looking at Gertrude as if she wanted to tell her something.

'We're going to check the last lot of fencing,' Tristan announced as he set his plate on the sink.

'Oh, that's fine, my dears. But Gertrude, I have some news for you.'

'Can it wait until we get back?' she asked.

'Yes, I suppose so. I have a letter from the orphanage.'

'Oh,' Gertrude didn't know what to do next. She was sure Summer was in danger. But it must be news about her parents. Had they been alive after all this time? She looked at Aunt Betty and then at Tristan, who had been waiting quietly by the door. He shrugged his shoulders as if to say it was up to her.

'We won't be long,' she said. She had to make a choice. And right now, her friend was more important; she was in danger.

Chapter 31

After shrinking as they entered Hollow Woods, Gertrude and Tristan said a quick hello to Gilmyer and raced to see Mortar and Logan. It was night at Hollow Woods confirming in some way to Gertrude that the scry she saw was real. They found Mortar and Logan in the Throne Room. Mortar sat upright on his throne with Tutu perched above him. Logan was pacing the length of the room looking distressed.

'Where's Summer?' was the first thing Gertrude said as they entered.

'She has been missing for two moons,' answered Logan, a puzzled look forming on his face.

'Did you know she was missing?' asked Tutu.

'I was practicing scrying. Last night I had a vision

of her. Her hands were bound, and she was in what looked like a cave. But the person she was with I haven't seen before.'

Gertrude's concerns were correct. She needed to know how to use the stones more effectively to help find Summer. Tutu was the only one who understood the scrying stones. He could help her through her visions.

'Assemble the guard,' Mortar demanded. Gertrude watched as one of the guards ran off. She had hoped she was wrong about Summer.

'What did this person look like?' asked Logan.

'The scry was weak. But I think he would have been taller than Mortar. He was wearing a hooded cloak, and his hair was long and grey.'

'That could describe many of our elders,' said Tutu.

'Oh, and he had a large triangle tattooed on his hand.'

Mortar looked at Tutu, then Logan, and then back at Gertrude.

'No, it can't be. It's impossible!' said Mortar.

'No, it's not,' returned Tutu.

'What?' both Tristan and Logan said.

'Folmar has escaped,' said Tutu. 'The scrolls tell of a way to break out of the Eternal Prism, but I just can't recall how.'

Gertrude had been trying to piece together what all of this meant and whether any of the incidents were connected.

'Did Baxter return,' she asked. She remembered how Baxter led them to The Darkness. Logan hadn't thought Baxter could stoop to what he had tried to do to them.

'That's it,' Tutu blurted out. He fluttered the length of the room and back again, looking like he had solved the puzzle.

'What's it,' said Logan.

'The only way out of the Eternal Prism is to enter a host. The host must have a weak or broken heart.'

'Baxter,' said Mortar. He suddenly looked pale and took in a deep breath. 'Send the guards to find Baxter,' he shouted, anger now filling him.

Gertrude, Tristan, and Tutu were sent to scour the

scrolls and see what power or remedy they could find to help save Summer and Baxter. Tutu fluttered from shelf to shelf in what remained of the fire-ravished library. In places that once held a mound of scrolls now resembled the pit like a fireplace. Gertrude was disheartened to see such a waste of knowledge and history for the elves and The Four Lands.

'I know it's here somewhere,' Tutu said more to himself than anyone else. 'Here, grab this one, for me, Tristan, and lay it on the table would you.'

Tristan obeyed Tutu, and he still got a kick out the fact that the bird could talk.

'What are you looking for?' asked Gertrude.

'Any script or symbols that relates to the Eternal Prism and a host.'

Tristan had unrolled the scroll along the length of the table and let the rest of it spew down onto the marble floor. Gertrude started looking at the information at the end of the scroll while Tristan concentrated in the middle.

Though Gertrude didn't understand the language properly, there some words she did recognise which helped decipher some of script. 'Look, I think I've found something.' Tutu flew from the table to the floor to have a look at what Gertrude had found. Tutu read in silence and kept umming and nodding to himself.

'Well. What does it say?' asked Tristan.

'I was afraid this would be the case.'

'What is it?' said Gertrude.

'The rule of the Eternal Prism states what I said earlier. The prisoner can escape using a series of chants, but only when there is an eclipse which isn't very often mind you.'

'And' said Tristan.

'And according to the rules, the way to remove Folmar from his host which has to be Baxter is to kill the host.'

'No. we can't do that,' said Tristan.

'There doesn't seem to be a choice,' replied Tutu.

Gertrude pondered what Tutu had just said and wondered why Baxter or Folmar would want Summer.

'What do you think Folmar wants with Summer?'

'I believe he plans to kill her to stop the union of her and Logan. He would have this knowledge through Baxter's memories past and present.'

'We have to stop him. Them,' said Tristan.

'But we don't know where they are,' said Gertrude, a new wave of worry washing over her.

'You might be wrong,' replied Tutu.

'What do you mean,' asked Gertrude.

'You have already seen where she is through the stones.'

'But I'm not very good at it.'

'Try it, it can't hurt, can it,' said Tristan.

Gertrude dragged the stones from her pocket and placed them on the marble floor in front of her. She didn't know how she would be able to relax like Summer had shown her, knowing Summer's life was at risk.

'Give me room.' She waved her hands at Tutu and Tristan, and they backed away. 'And stop staring. I need to focus.'

'Rightio,' replied Tristan trying his hardest to look away.

Tutu and Tristan sat quietly on the floor near Gertrude. 'Tutu, I need you to guide me through the scry. I've only had one lesson with Summer and have been practicing while back on the farm. I'm not very good at it,' she repeated.

'Of course, I will. But I think you're better at it then you think. Grab those cushion Tristan, and put them behind Gertrude.'

That gave Gertrude a little burst of confidence.

'Come on, get on with it,' said Tristan.

'Shh, I need to concentrate.' Gertrude closed her eyes.

'Now clear your mind,' suggested Tutu. 'And take a few deep breaths, in and out to release any built-up tension. That's it.'

Gertrude could feel her mind clearing. The emptiness before the scry. She opened her eyes and looked deep into the ruby stones. She thought of Summer over and over in her mind. The stones glowed and swirled with light brighter than before.

'Wow,' said Tristan. Tutu stifled Tristan outburst with his expanded wing avoiding a break from the scry.

Gertrude sat, staring at the stones for a long time before she broke the scry. Tears fell down her cheeks.

'They are on a mound of some kind.'

Chapter 32

Summer's throat was parched from lack of water and trying to talk Baxter out of what he was about to do. She saw glimpses of Folmar pushing through as he took over Baxter's body.

There was no escape. Folmar had bound her hands. And he had cast some sort of spell that stopped her from moving. She was in a small alcove, a rock shelter that sat on the left of the Sacred Mound. She was cold and tired and hoped Logan would find her soon.

It had been two moons, and no one had come for her. She believed if she couldn't get through to Baxter that she would be resting in death before dawning. She had seen a glimmer of hope a while ago when she was reminiscing about their childhood they shared before Baxter's mother lay in death.

But then nothing. It was as if Folmar was strangling Baxter from the inside. She had worked out what Folmar was planning. The Scared Mound held the key to the shield which protected Hollows Woods, and The Four Lands from the outside. It was like an invisible dome. If this dome was lifted, not only would they be exposed to the human world, but it would also see the extinction of all The Four Lands. The humans didn't know of their existence. And haven't known for over three hundred years. That was all about to change.

Summer also knew why Folmar had taken her instead of just waiting for them all to perish. He wanted Mortar and his family to suffer. As he suffered. Locked in the Eternal Prism, forevermore. He wanted revenge and killing Summer would give that to him.

The mound was over five leagues wide. Grass and bushes sat on the slopes which surrounded it. The west side was a sheer cliff that fell to rocky terrain. Close to that edge was the key to the dome. To anyone else it looked like an upright stone-shaped pillar. It was no rounder than two stretched-out hands and only waist-high. It could only be moved by a series of chants over a period of two moons. And could only be activated at first light of dawning.

Summer had learned of the destruction activation from when Tutu had taught her and her friends the history of Hollow Woods many moons ago. But she didn't think that any of the people that populated The Four Lands would ever want to destroy it.

Summer knew the dawning was close, and she tried so hard to stay awake. She racked her brain trying to figure out a way to stop Folmar. She had the ability to send a message with her mind, but Folmar had thought of every possibility, and the spell he had cast left her mind weak. When Baxter had approached her, she thought it was Logan. Baxter had run off and hadn't been seen since the meeting of The Four Lands, where he was denounced from his right as leader.

Baxter had said he had a surprise, which is something Logan often did with Summer. Before she had a chance to alert Logan, Folmar had cast his spell.

Folmar stood in front of the key for a long-time chanting. But now he came back to where Summer was in the darkened cave. He dragged her to a standing position and pushed her towards the key and the cliff.

She wasn't sure what he would do to her. Would he cast a final deadly spell? Or would he simply throw her from the cliff to her death?

Folmar had removed the stillness spell to enable him to move Summer. Summer saw it as an opportunity to escape. But where to? It was many leagues before she could use the bushes and grass on the slope to hide in. But she had to try. She had to escape! She had to live!

Summer stopped resisting but instead acted as though she had weakened, putting more weight on Folmar.

'What are you doing?'

'I'm exhausted, Baxter. Please can't we stop a while?' Summer had never let Folmar know she could see him showing through and taking over Baxter's body.

'I suppose I can give you one last request before you meet the other side of life.' Folmar loosened his grip, and Summer rested on the grassy slope. She had to keep the pretence up for just a bit long. She was just about to slide out of his grip, but he tightened it. 'That's enough rest for you. The Dawning is coming.'

Summer stayed limp and a deadweight hoping that would give her more time. Folmar had to time it right for his plan to work. Maybe she can save Hollow Woods? She just had to stop him from reaching for the key.

'Stop it,' he shouted. 'I won't have the likes of you ruin the destiny of The Four Lands.'

'Please, Baxter, please don't do this.' Folmar started to push Summer. She tried with all her might to push back, but he was too strong. This can't be how it all ends, she thought.

Chapter 33

'Come with me. I know where Folmar is. And Tristan, get your bow and arrows. We'll meet you in the courtyard. Hurry, it's almost Dawning,' said Tutu.

'Where are they,' asked Gertrude. Tutu flew ahead with Gertrude having to run to keep up.

'Folmar is up on the Sacred Mount. He is about to destroy Hollow Woods and The Four Lands.'

'Shouldn't we find Mortar and Logan?'

'There is no time. Have you got your Emblem of Peace?'

'Yes, but…'

Once Tristan returned, they followed Tutu to the west of Hollow Woods and down through a series of tunnels before coming out the over side, east of the Sacred Mound.

'Shh,' said Tutu. They could see Folmar pushing Summer towards the key and the cliff. They took cover behind a series of bushes.

'What now? When will Mortar and Logan be here?' asked Tristan.

'They won't be. It's up to us,' replied Tutu in a low voice.

'What? What do you mean?' said Tristan.

'What I mean is, you need to kill Baxter.'

Tristan shook his head. 'I can't kill Baxter.'

'It is the only way, dear boy.'

'But I've never killed anything before. Not even an ant.'

'Tristan, we have to save Hollow Woods and Summer,' said Gertrude.

'Can you get him from here?' asked Tutu.

Tristan looked towards Baxter. Next, he licked his finger and stuck it in the air to check the direction of wind. 'It's quite a long way.'

'Yes, but can you do it,' said Tutu.

'Yes, I think I can.'

Gertrude was worried about Summer. What if

Tristan shot her instead of Baxter? She watched as Summer struggled to delay Folmar from carrying out his plot. Summer was pushing back on Folmar making it difficult for him to push her.

'What now, Tutu?' said Gertrude.

'Now, as soon as Tristan aims and shoots the arrow, count to five slowly. Then run as fast as you can and a little to the left of Tristan's line of sight. Once the arrow hits Folmar, move Summer out of danger, and you will them perform the ancient chant to restore Hollow Woods.'

'Me?'

'Yes, you, Gertrude.' Tutu nodded. 'You can and must. It's told by the moon's shadow. You know the chant, and you hold the Emblem of Peace. And remember. Sing the chant with a loving heart.'

Gertrude wasn't sure how any of this was going to work. How could two children save Hollow Woods? But Tutu had confidence in her and Tristan. And besides there was no time to find Mortar and Logan.

'Hurry. Look, the dawning is upon us. Are you ready, Tristan?'

Tristan nodded and aimed the arrow at Baxter. Baxter had his back to Tristan, which made the shot difficult. Tristan aimed for the left and in below the shoulders. Straight for the heart. He took a deep breath, and as he exhaled, he released the arrow.

Gertrude counted slowly to five and ran as fast as she could. She watched in horror as Baxter faulted when the arrow hit him. He turned and staggered but kept a tight grip on Summer. Gertrude met his eyes.

He turned back around and continued. The arrow must have missed. Gertrude stopped, cupped her hands, and yelled, 'Again, Tristan.' She stood her distance until she saw the arrow fly past and hit Baxter another time. She watched as he fell to his knees and released his grip on Summer.

Gertrude saw her opportunity to grab Summer and pulled her away from Baxter. Baxter lay on his side, moaning. In the short time Gertrude had moved Summer to a safer spot, Tutu and Tristan had reached her side.

'Hurry start your chant. Place the emblem on the key,' said Tutu.

To Gertrude's surprise, the rock pillar was etched out in the shape of The Emblem of Peace. It fitted perfectly. She took in a breath and sang.

> *The Moon it rides above the wind,*
> *To ensure the earth is well aligned.*
> *The Tulips bring our season in,*
> *And welcome in our next of kin.*
> *The Sun warms our hearts,*
> *And guides us through the Ancient charts.*
> *Bring this combination to accord,*
> *Hollow Woods to be restored.*

Strange cracks were forming in the sky. It sounded like thunder. It wasn't working.

'Keep singing,' commanded Tutu.

Gertrude found it hard to stay focused with all the noise. More and more cracks appeared. She closed her eyes and thought about her mother and father and how much she loved them. And she sang the chant over and over until she realised the noise, the cracks had stopped.

She opened her eyes to see that Mortar, Logan, and the guards had arrived. And at that very moment they witnessed Folmar escape Baxter's body and float away.

Mortar rushed to Baxter, kneeled on the ground, and pulled his son's limp body to him. Tristan slowly moved towards Mortar and put his arm on his shoulder.

'I'm sorry, Mortar.' That was all he could say. But now he had seen Folmar leave Baxter's body; he knew he had done the right thing.

Chapter 34

Gertrude and Tristan were heading back to the Appleton Farm for a well-earned rest. And besides that, the people of Hollow Woods and particularly Mortar and Logan needed time to mourn the loss of Baxter. Gertrude was eager to know what the letter from the orphanage was about. Was it news that her parents were alive? It has been too long. She didn't want her hopes up. But now, what if her parents were alive? What if they weren't? What was going to happen next?

She had pushed her feelings aside. Her friends in Hollow Woods had needed her. She was glad about the decision she had made after her vision through the scrying stones.

Mortar, though truly devastated, was kind to

Tristan and reassured him he had acted in the best interest of Hollow Woods. Without his and Gertrude's help, no living being would have survived. Summer was also full of praise, and she was elated Gertrude had found her through the scrying stones.

Gertrude noticed Tristan's unusual silence as they approached the barn.

'Are you all, right?'

Tristan stopped in his tracks. 'I killed Baxter.'

Gertrude put her arm around his shoulder and dragged him closer.

'But look at all the lives you saved. You're a hero, Tristan. You, the boy from the orphanage, a hero.'

Tristan half-smiled. 'But I see it over and over in my head; it won't leave me.'

'Come on, let's go and help Aunt Betty bake some scones. That might help cheer you up.'

Gertrude remembered the first day she had met Tristan on the train. He was so different now. He had grown taller and filled out. He even had muscles from all the training he had done with Logan. He wasn't clumsy anymore and had a confidence about him, though he was still funny.

Aunt Betty was sitting at the kitchen table drinking tea with Mr. James. Tristan sniffed the air. 'Scones.'

"It looks like we don't have to make them after all,' said Gertrude.

'Well, you two were quick at checking the fencing. Is it all in order?'

'Yes, but one pole will need replacing in a month or two,' answered Tristan.

Gertrude and Tristan took a seat and helped themselves to the pile of scones sitting in the middle of the table.

'You're doing a fine job, boy, looking after the farm. I wouldn't have guessed when I first laid eyes on you,' said Mr. James.

'Thank you, I think.'

'I was just telling your Aunt Betty I'll be selling up my farm. I'm too old to keep it running.'

'Oh, we'll miss you,' said Gertrude.

'How will we get to Sunday church?' asked Tristan.

'Whenever have you like going to church?' Aunt Betty queried.

Tristan scratched his head. 'Never. But I was thinking about you, Aunt Betty.'

Aunt Betty pondered his reply. 'Firstly, my friend, Doris, and her husband have offered to take us to church, that's until you are competent with your driving. Mr. James is leaving his truck here for you, and he'll give you a few lessons before he leaves.'

'Wow, thanks, Mr. James. I can't image myself driving down the road in an automobile.' Tristan was truly exciting about owning a vehicle and someday driving it but didn't like the part where he still had to go to church.

'I'll see you in a week for your first lesson in the field. No harm can be done there. I best be off.' Mr. James stood, grabbing his hat, which sat on the table.

Tristan stood at the same time and hugged Mr. James.

***

Tristan and Gertrude helped Aunt Betty clear the table and wash the dishes. Gertrude had been waiting for the right time to ask Aunt Betty about the letter. She waited patiently while Mr. James was visiting. She was itching to know what it said. She missed her parents terribly. At the same time, she liked it here with Aunt Betty, Tristan, Carmel the cow, and her friends at Hollow Woods.

'Can you tell me what's in the letter,' Gertrude blurted out. She wiped the last cup and placed it in the cupboard.

'Yes, well. Come with me.'

Gertrude followed her into the living room and sat on the lounge chair under the window. Aunt Betty sat opposite in her large comfortable recliner. Tristan hung about the doorway, not knowing what to do.

'Come on, Tristan,' Gertrude said. 'Whatever is in this letter might affect you in some way.' Gertrude had grown fond for Tristan and now considered him more of a brother than a bother. Though, sometimes he could still be annoying.

Tristan sat on the floor close to Gertrude. They leaned forward in anticipation as Aunt Betty dragged the neatly folded letter from her apron pocket. Aunt Betty cleared her throat, unfolded the letter, and wiped her eyes with her handkerchief.

Gertrude could see this was upsetting to Aunt Betty. *Could that mean my parents are still alive?*

'Right, this is what the governess has informed us.'

Dear Mrs. Appleton,

You will be pleased to know that we have located Gertrude's, Aunt Gwen Higgins. Who had escaped the bombing by moving to Venice and has now returned. She is happy to take the child in until she turns sixteen. She will correspond with you directly and arrange the transportation of the child back to Britania.

Further, Ms. Higgin has informed me that the bodies of the child's parents have not been found.

Sincerely

Ms. Bolding

Governess East Side Orphanage.

Gertrude's eyes had started to blur as the last part of the letter was read. She so hoped she could be with her parents again. Tears fell uninhibited into her lap soaking her clothes. Neither Tristan nor Aunt Betty moved or said a word. They sat there waiting for Gertrude to take in the news.

Gertrude had not cried like this since she was placed in the orphanage. And she had soon learned by the swish of the governess' stick to keep her emotions to herself. But it was different here; she felt she could be who she was supposed to be.

She never liked her Aunt Gwen. And she remembered a time when she was about four years old, and Aunt Gwen was watching over her while her parents enjoyed a rare outing together. The whole time she had sat in the parlour reading, drinking wine in the middle of the day, and had invited strangers into the house. Gertrude wasn't offered anything to eat or drink for the entire day, though she had asked. That had been the last time she had seen her aunt.

Gertrude wiped her eyes. 'I'm staying here. I want to stay here.'

About the Author

Wendy Haynes completed a Diploma in Creative Writing at Southern Cross University. Her writing focuses on middle-grade fantasy, historical, and contemporary stories for children, picture books, junior fiction, and YA.

Her first picture book This book along with her first picture book – Hayden's Bedtime is on the NSW Premier's Reading Challenge list. She is available for school visits.

You can find Wendy here:

https://www.facebook.com/inprintpublishing/

'But Tutu said the stones never lie.'

While practicing the ancient form of scrying with her ruby red stones, Gertrude views a goblin girl in the woods. Who is she? And why can Gertrude see her? Is there more trouble brewing in Hollow Woods? Join Gertrude and Tristan on another journey through the door in the woods. They soon learn the Evil High Elf Folmar has a plan that could start another civil war between the citizens of the Four Land – the Elves, Dwarfs, Goblins and the Trolls. But Gertrude's new skills may help conquer Folmar once and for all. Can they stop the war or are they too late?

Also by the Author

A FUN RHYMING BEDTIME STORY for 3 - 6 year olds gives you and your child the opportunity to explore bedtime rituals and discover with Hayden's and his dad what's behind the DOOR, under the BED, inside the CUPBOARD, and in the DRAWER. Hayden's Bedtime offers a positive bedtime routine for children who are feeling scared at bedtime and need that extra comfort.

Excellent for beginning and early readers, it is easy to read, a fun exploration of language, and a relaxing read with cute images for younger readers.

www.ingramcontent.com/pod-product-compliance
Lightning Source LLC
LaVergne TN
LVHW041614070426
835507LV00008B/225